MW01128132

This book is a work of fiction. The names, characters, places, and incidents are products of the writer's imagination or have been used fictitiously and are not to be construed as real. Any resemblance to persons, living or dead, actual events, locale or organizations is entirely coincidental.

Other titles in this series:
All Knighter
Heat of the Knight

Sean Knight is second in command of Knight Ops, a special task force that's quickly gaining more notoriety than Seal Team Six. While Sean enjoys showing off his tactical skills on life-threatening missions, he also loves coming home to Louisiana to relax and do some catfishin'... and hunting for sexy females to warm his bed.

But the mysterious Creole woman he wants isn't interested in his bed—because she's working alongside him to find a missing nuclear warhead.

When six-feet-two inches of sexy steel in camo walks into Elise's office and decrees she's working with him, she knows Sean is the type of man she wants to avoid. Though their late nights spent cracking codes are making it hard to stay on task. Who can blame her when Sean Knight is packing heat in all the best ways? While their work takes priority, she can't help but think deciphering Sean is worth her while, especially when the hard-ass man admits that lately he's been wondering how it feels to be with a woman who actually cares if he returns home safe after these dangerous missions.

Heat of the Knight

by

Em Petrova

Chapter One

"This SOB is fast." Ben's huffed words filled Sean's earpiece and ratcheted his heart rate up five notches.

Missing out on a foot chase when you were late joining your special ops unit was frowned upon in the military. And when the commander was your big brother, the outcome was even worse. He was in for a world of shit for this, and all for a woman.

"Heading east. I have the agent in sight. Keep your heads on a swivel." Ben's update was followed by several grunts of agreement from the rest of the team.

Sean slammed the pedal of his old El Camino to the floor and gunned it through the New Orleans streets. The city was quieter at this hour, unusual in this area. He didn't like it—his sixth sense was blaring like an alarm during an air strike.

"C'mon," he urged his baby, smoothing his hand over the leather-wrapped steering wheel. Not half an hour before, he'd been stroking a woman into peak after peak. Getting the summons from Knight Ops was the kiss of

1

death for a relationship, and this was the second time he'd walked out on some very dirty bedroom play with Ali.

But he'd jumped out of bed, at the ready. While throwing on clothes and hopping behind the wheel, he never thought the Knight Ops team would be able to locate a Russian spy who'd evaded captivity for a decade. Yet they'd found him in their own back yard and had eyes on him.

"Heading northeast now. Past Creole Joe's." Ben's words came in his normal voice, and the only sign Sean had that he was sprinting was the small hiccup of air between words.

Sean took in his surroundings. Creole Joe's was a few blocks over, and he could head the Russian off.

Without bothering with turn signals, he took a bend at top speed. His left front tire rolled up over the curb but came down smoothly, barely jarring him. He ran a hand over the steering wheel, giving it the caress of affection it deserved. His car might be circa '78 but it outperformed many modern models. And looked cool as hell.

"Closing the gap. Ninja, you got him in view?" Ben asked.

A laugh sounded. "Since when are you calling me Ninja?" their youngest brother Roades asked.

"Quit fucking around and answer the question, dickhead."

Another laugh from Roades. "The agent is not in sight, Captain."

"Dammit. You and Dylan must be off course."

"We're not off course," Dylan put in. "We know these streets like we know our own dicks, sir."

More laughter from the other guys, who were fanned across the five-block area, by the sounds of it. Still, Sean was the closest. And he had a six-cylinder.

A flash of something caught his eye and he veered left just as the man they were chasing hurdled a fire hydrant feet away from Sean. He screeched to a stop and threw the car in park, hitting the ground running. The Russian might be fast, but so was he.

Pumping his arms close to his body to generate speed, he gained on the man. The guy threw a wild look over his shoulder, and in that second Sean knew he'd do anything to escape. He was a wild animal, cornered by the people who'd ship him to his mother country, where he'd be up on charges on his failure to execute his mission and looked in the eyes before being shot for letting down his commanders. If he stayed in the US, he'd only find himself imprisoned for life under top security.

He threw himself forward and hit the man from behind, launching them both onto the pavement. The air hung with the scent of yeast from the nearby bakery, but Sean's nose flooded with the reek of sweat and fear.

"Don't fucking move," he growled as he whipped the man's wrists together, and with one jerk of his hand, bound them with a zip-tie he preferred to rope. Easier to carry and you could make them as tight as you needed.

"You got me out of the bed of a very beautiful woman, asshole, and I'm not going to go easy on you," he said to the man glaring up at him from one eye. He tightened the tie until the flesh swelled around the plastic – he couldn't risk the guy getting free.

"I got him on the ground," he said to his team.

"What the fuck? Thunder?" His brother Chaz sounded stunned.

"No, it's Santa Clause. Did you assholes think I'd abandon you?" He kept a knee in the man's back. "Name," he demanded.

"Fuck off." Damn, the guy's English was better than his own. No wonder he'd managed to fit in undetected in this country for a decade.

Using only a portion of his strength, Sean hauled the man to his feet. "Walk nicely now. I don't want to have to take out my weapon. Then again, you did fuck up a very enjoyable experience."

When the man didn't budge, Sean kicked his Achilles. The Russian groaned and slowly trundled forward.

Sean led the criminal to the back of the El Camino and depressed a button to raise the tonneau cover over the truck bed. The cover lifted, revealing a tool box big enough to fit a man.

The Russian tensed. "You don't plan to put me in there, do you?"

He looked over the Russian's physique. Yeah, he'd fit, no problem.

Sean contemplated the scars on his face, probably put there by the people he'd failed. Yet there were more open areas of skin than scars, which meant he'd had a successful career. Now it was at an end.

"Yes, I fucking do intend to put you in there. Did you think you were getting a cushy ride to the airport?" He dragged the man a few more inches to the back of the vehicle and pushed up the lid of the toolbox. "See? Lots of space. Breathing room, we'll call it. Except you'll be gagged." He one-handedly removed a bandana from his back pocket, ignoring the faint whiff of perfume clinging to the fibers.

"Smells like a cheap whore," the Russian spat before Sean stuffed it in his mouth.

He glared at the spy, who stood two inches shorter. "Not nice to talk about a lady like that. Now get in the box."

He stood there unmoving just as Ben and Chaz careened around the corner and skidded to a stop by the El Camino.

"Now it's three against one and you don't have use of your hands. I know you don't like those odds. Get in the box." Sean's voice grated with authority.

Ben and Chaz closed in, reaching for the Russian. Chaz used a short bungee cord around his mouth to hold in the bandana Sean had stuffed inside. Then the two lifted him bodily and dropped him into the box.

Sean stared at the man impassively. In the past few months he'd been part of Operation Freedom Flag Southern US division, or OFFSUS, he'd seen and done some wild shit, but this guy deserved far worse than transport in his toolbox.

Sean moved to close the lid, but the man kept his ankle on the edge. "Move it or I'll smash it. We weren't told to deliver you whole — just alive."

So much hate burned from the man's eyes as Sean bound his feet as well.

"You never told me your name," Sean said in a deadly, low Russian with a perfect accent. The guy's eyes widened minutely at Sean's use of his native tongue. "But you don't need to. Say goodnight, Aleksandr Polakoff."

He slammed the lid and turned to his brothers and fellow teammates.

Ben raked his fingers through his hair. "Jesus, Sean."

Without a word, Sean circled to the driver's side and got behind the wheel. Through the open window, he heard Ben giving Chaz orders to meet up with the rest of the team and follow. Then Ben slid in, riding shotgun.

Sean pulled into the street.

"Where the hell have you been?" Ben demanded.

"Occupied. Won't happen again, Captain." He really did feel damn bad that Knight Ops had begun this mission without him, solely because he couldn't untie Ali, make sure she was okay, *and* dress and arrive in time.

"Damn straight you will, or I'll have you court martialed and shot." Ben's tone was the no-nonsense bark of a captain, not a big brother. And Sean couldn't blame him. The team's success and safety depended on them all doing their jobs.

"I know it's all bluff." Sean shot him a sidelong look.

Ben didn't glance away from the windshield. "Try me."

Silence descended as they rolled through the Louisiana streets, the lights of businesses switched off and leaving only shadowed storefronts.

"Why the hell was Polakoff in the Big Easy anyway?" Sean asked after a spell.

"Who the hell knows. Must be meeting someone."

"Who tipped off OFFSUS?"

Ben lifted a shoulder and let it fall. The action could be a shrug or Ben's signature move when he felt uncomfortable about answering a question. Not unusual in the Knight family, considering their positions.

"Guess we'll hear it all when we debrief."

"Yeah." Ben sat silent for another block or two. Finally, he said, "So how tall was she?"

Sean grinned. "A gentleman never talks." His mind was thick with images of the sultry

Ali, long-limbed and strung up, about to be seduced out of her pretty little mind. He'd been seeing her for a month or so, and to say their nights were hot was like calling a Marine a wimp.

"You bringing her to the cabin this weekend?"

Now it was time for Sean to shift his shoulders in a semblance of an uncommitted shrug. While he'd been considering taking Ali to the family cabin to meet his *maman* and *pére,* he wasn't sure they were at that level yet. Besides, Knights were playboys, not known for settling down.

"I've thought about bringing her," he said finally. "If the family is actually at the cabin, that is." The Knight brothers were first and foremost defenders of their country. While based in the South, they still found themselves flown off the grid at times, gaining more notoriety than Seal Team 6 the past few months.

"Yeah, might not be a good idea to bring her just yet."

Sean nodded, eyes directed on the road leading to the base where they'd unload the baggage in the back.

"You did good back there, Sean. But you know I have to tell Jackson that you were late to the scene."

He grunted. "Second in command's usually the fuck-up, so he'll be expecting it."

The gates opened, and he rolled through, followed by the black SUV carrying the rest of the team. The next hours consisted of an exhaustive and exhausting debriefing. When Colonel Jackson got Sean alone, the intimidating officer gave him the cold stare that typically made a Marine's gonads crawl inside and seek shelter.

Standing at attention, Sean stared back.

"At ease, Knight. I hear you were late to the party."

"With all respect, sir, I *was* the party. I captured Polakoff."

He narrowed his eyes at Sean. "You Knight brothers are all the same—mouthy. Your parents raise you to be mouthy, Knight?"

"No, sir. Had my mouth washed out with soap more days than I can count."

Colonel Jackson grunted. "That El Camino's pretty damn good for hauling prisoners."

He grinned. "Yes, sir."

Long seconds passed. Sean had been sized up many times in his lifetime, and he knew when a man was assessing him. Colonel Jackson was damn good at making a Marine shake in his boots, if Sean was the boot-shaking type.

"What do you want for yourself, Knight?"

He blinked. "Sir?"

"What are your goals? And you better not give me that bullshit Ben did when he said he wanted to golf, fish and fuck."

Sean smirked. "I love me some catfishin', sir. Can't deny it." His Cajun drawl was even more pronounced when talking about the things he loved.

"Catfishin'. Hmm. I'd say you love hunting the ladies too." He gave Sean's shoulder a sniff. "Do you have aspirations of having your own team someday?"

He jolted. "My own team?"

"Leading your own team. Taking control."

Mind whirling, Sean wondered if the colonel had learned to dig into a man's psyche or if he was in this superior position because he knew how to do it. Since his second tour, Sean had thought of pushing for that top spot in the food chain, but since being recruited to OFFSUS, he hadn't given it much thought.

"You're damn good at strategy, Knight."

"Thank you, sir."

"There might be something opening up for you in the months to come. Be sure your tardiness doesn't hamper that. Dismissed."

11

Sean gave a stiff salute, but his heart was pounding out of time. His own team? Leading men of his own?

He walked out of Jackson's office and started down the corridor. Dylan suddenly flanked him. "Okay, bro?"

"Yeah." He held out his fisted hand and Dylan brushed his knuckles against his. Sean had to get out of here. Besides needing to think on Jackson's words, he had a beautiful woman who deserved a finish to what they'd started.

"Does Ben need anything else, because I'm going to jam."

"Nah, go on. She shouldn't be kept waiting." Dylan raised his chin in farewell to Sean and dropped back to speak with Chaz, who was emerging from another office.

As Sean sailed through the streets to reach Ali, he didn't think about the spy who'd occupied the toolbox just hours before. He could only think of one thing—a certain sultry vixen.

At her place, he used the key she'd shown him hidden among a potted fern and let himself in. The place was silent, dark. His balls ached in anticipation, fueled by the adrenaline rush of the mission he'd just completed.

Fucking after a battle was a high unlike any other, and even if she had no clue what he did for a living, she could benefit from his adrenaline woody.

He pushed open the bedroom door and peeked in. His breath caught at the sight of her legs in the air… and another man balls-deep in his girl.

Ali looked over the man's shoulder at Sean and gasped, trying to scramble into another, less raunchy position. But it was too late—Sean's emotions were already switched off.

"Oh my God, Sean!"

He only stared at her face, not giving a fuck what the other man looked like. "Guess I'm not taking you home to *Maman*." He twisted away.

"Wait, Sean. I didn't think you were coming back."

He kept walking, his heart a block of ice. "That's exactly the problem." He tossed her key on the coffee table on the way past and slammed the door behind him.

As he got behind the wheel of his El Camino, he realized why he'd told Ben he wasn't ready to bring her to the cabin—the connection wasn't strong enough. He had no idea what a true relationship should feel like, but having a woman eager for him to return was number one on his list.

Plenty of women out there were eager and supportive. Hell, Ben's woman Dahlia had tracked him down and hopped a flight to New York City to be with him the night before they flew out on one of the most dangerous missions Sean had ever survived. There would be plenty more like it... but who would be here to give a damn if he returned?

* * * * *

Elise walked into her bedroom wrapped in a silky robe and came face-to-face with the six-foot-three-inch wall of muscle that was her ex-husband.

"What the hell are you doing in my bedroom?" The words came out as resigned. Since this happened all the time, she *was* resigned. She moved past his chiseled flesh and started toward her walk-in closet.

"I like what you've done with the decorating." Bo, aka Robert Hawkings, known as Hawk to his team of special ops agents working with homeland security, waved at her surroundings. "It doesn't look anything like you, but I like it."

"Thanks. I think." She'd changed the space to reflect her personal tastes. On the outside, she was a hard-nosed special operator for the US government, but at night she wanted to shuck off her tough persona and crawl into her big white shabby chic bed with the flowered quilts and ruffled pillowcases. Her lamp was antique glass and the shade sported pompoms that Bo flicked with a fingertip.

"So you know what you have to do, Elise?" Bo followed her into her closet. She dropped her robe and stood in only bra and panties. Wearing such sexy garments in the presence of any other man than her ex-husband would be dangerous to her mission of actually leaving the house and intercepting this message. But she and Bo had an understanding.

She drew two dresses off the hanging bar, a red and a black, and held them up for him. "Which one?"

"Red. It hugs your ass better." He spoke without a bit of heat in his tone. Dressing in front of him was like hanging out with a buddy in the locker room, shooting the breeze after a workout.

She put the black dress back on the bar and removed the red one from the hanger. Stepping into it, she said, "Of course I know what I have to do."

"Find the blonde. Remember, she's five-nine." He eyed Elise as if sizing up if she and this blonde would fit together.

"You're a sick fucker, you know that, Bo? I'm not finding the blonde to make out with her."

15

"If you do, make sure you get video."

She rolled her eyes. He'd always found two girls going at it to be hot—typical man with coed cheerleader fantasies. Elise had never been into it, which was just one of many things they did not have in common. Why she'd ever married him was always a question mark in her mind.

Then again, they *did* work well together. Paired on a case, they were unstoppable. Somehow that had translated into a relationship that never should have happened. They were much better as partners and dare she say it? Friends.

She turned, presenting her back to him. "Zip me up."

He did so without the lingering touches of a former lover or a man who had interest in anything about her besides ensuring she followed his orders. She spun to face him again and found he had two pairs of high heels chosen for her and sitting side by side on the carpet.

"I prefer the silver," he said.

"They pinch my toes. I'll go with the black."

"Good choice. You have to be able to run in them."

She met his gaze. Damn, he was a handsome son of a bitch. Tall, dashing, with dark eyes that could bruise they looked so deeply. It was no wonder she'd fallen for him, and now he seemed determined to sleep with as many women as possible just to prove he could.

Not that Elise cared.

She slipped on the black heels with a cluster of rhinestones on the toes. "Jewelry?"

"Nothing too flashy."

She grinned. "If I didn't know better, I'd think you're gay."

"The term is metrosexual. A man who loves clothes doesn't have to be gay. Now. Repeat your instructions."

She rolled her eyes and went to her bedroom to rummage through her jewelry. Bo followed, his heavy combat boots and dark clothing looking out of place in her frilly bedroom.

"I go to the party. I find the blonde. Not to have a pillow fight with her," she added when he grinned. "I watch who she speaks to and then I intercept any messages."

"What if it's not written on paper? If nothing is exchanged?"

She reached into her bra and pulled out a bug device no bigger than the head of a pin. "I bump into her—stop looking at me that way, you pervert—and plant this. Then I listen to the conversations she has." She looped a rhinestone necklace over her head. "I'll have the code cracked and be home eating that new pint of Ben and Jerry's by midnight."

"And what's your backup plan if that doesn't work?"

"I use my firmware to clone her phone. No one is immune to hacking."

Bo drifted closer to her. "Good. Your perfume smells great. Always loved it. But tell me what you'll do if you're made."

Giving him a blank stare, she said, "Then I use the Smith and Wesson strapped to my thigh."

"Damn, girl. Let me see." He reached for her hem.

She batted him away. "I can handle this, Bo. Now do I look like I fit into this event?"

He assessed her, dark eyes roving from her shiny waves to her stilettos. "Perfectly. You know a lot's riding on you."

"Always is." She flashed him a grin and went on tiptoe to kiss his beard-roughened cheek. "Eww. You need a shave."

"The ladies eat up the five o'clock shadow." He waggled his brows.

18

"TMI. Okay, I'm off." She grabbed her small black evening bag that held breath mints and a passport in case things really went south.

At the door, Bo caught her by the elbow and swung her back to face him. "Be careful, Elise."

The warmth of having a friend like him on her side bloomed in her chest. They were always there for each other, even if they couldn't run a life together.

"I will. See you on the other side."

Chapter Two

"Holy shit. This is going to take months of work to crack." Elise shook her head at the information running over the computer screen.

"We don't have months." Her superior officer sat in shadows, which was fine because his disguise was nothing to look at. He appeared to be a middle-aged man with a receding hairline and glasses, though she guessed he didn't look like this at all. She only knew him as Hart.

"I'll do my best, work long hours. But I don't think I can get through all of this information in the time you need it."

"We'll get you help. But you have to understand how sensitive this information is. The message you intercepted was far beyond what we ever expected. This," he waved a hand at the screen, "is top priority."

She stared at the series of letters and numbers that seemed like simple notes to friends or even grocery lists but, carried to the wrong person, would be deadly to the US population. A thrill went through her—this was what she lived for, and she'd never had a project so big or important before.

Hart stood and she did too, keeping her post by the computer, eager to dig in. "I'll find you that help you need."

"Thank you, sir." She waited till the door closed behind him before dropping back into her seat. "Jesus," she breathed as she stared at the information. First thing she had to do was—

The door opened again, and she heard the familiar sound of Bo's boots. She barely glanced up as he hovered over her, a hand planted on the desk.

"You did amazing, Elise. This intel is invaluable."

"I know." She gave a small shake of her head. "And getting it was so easy too. It makes me wonder if they wanted us to find it."

"Like it's a decoy to throw us off?"

She nodded. But a string of words on the screen caught her eye, and her mind removed certain letters, rearranged, and came out with something else that had another meaning.

She reached for her keyboard and tapped out what she'd just cracked.

Bo released a low whistle. "Damn. I'll never stop being amazed by how your mind works. If only…"

She looked up into his eyes. "Yeah, we're better this way."

"Yeah."

Feeling an odd tension in her lower belly, she returned her attention to the screen. "I've got a lot of work to do, Bo."

"They're sending someone to help you." The tight tone of his voice roused her from the words on the screen. She studied the crease between his brows.

"Do you know who they're sending?"

"I can guess."

She arched a brow in a care-to-fill-me-in way.

A muscle leaped in the crease of his angular jaw. "Knight."

She blinked. "As in Knight Ops?"

"Yeah. One of the brothers is the one who hacked the Pentagon as a teen. Got recruited straight to working for the government and then got 'bored,' as it's told, and joined the Marines like his brothers."

"That kid is a Knight?"

"Yeah." He didn't look like he was stomaching it very well, and she wondered if his own cocky pride was threatened by men like the Knights who were gaining notoriety faster than any special ops team in the world.

Bo ran a hand over his face, creating a rasping noise. He still hadn't shaved and now that she looked closer, it appeared he hadn't gotten any sleep. Either he'd been occupied with one of his special lady friends or he'd been up all night waiting for news from her.

She pushed out a sigh. Their relationship was more complicated than she admitted to, but the bottom line was that love wasn't involved—at least not in the familiar sense of the word. She loved Bo like a best friend, if not a brother, though she could still admire how handsome he was. And how he was always there for her in all ways proved the depth of his feelings.

She'd do anything for him as well, and he knew it.

Resting a hand on his bulging forearm, she said, "You don't need to worry about me working with another guy. I can hold my own against the cockiest of men."

He laughed, even if it sounded far too gritty. He couldn't be… jealous, could he? No, of course not. He was just being protective of her, like a big brother over his younger sister.

"It's not you I'm worried about, Elise. I know you can grab a man by the balls, twist and pull faster than someone could lay hands on you. It's just…" He trailed off, looking into her eyes. "Forget it. I know you've got this." He stood and made for the door.

Typical man skirting the issues and running for his life.

No matter—she had work to do anyway. She turned back to the screen. Over her shoulder, she said, "Close the door behind you, Bo. I'll call you later."

He grunted but she ignored him, too engrossed in the challenge on the screen before her. She cracked her fingers and hovered the tips over the keyboard as her brain flooded with codes.

* * * * *

"Is that steak I smell burning on the grill?" Sean asked as he entered the kitchen.

"Oh damn!" His younger sister, Tyler, dashed for the back door and the deck where the grill was located.

"Tyler! You were supposed to keep watch on the steaks!" their mother called after her.

Sean crossed the kitchen and dropped a kiss to his *maman's* cheek. "Sorry I'm late."

She compressed her lips and gave him the eye, letting him know he wasn't getting anything past the woman who'd raised him. Not that he expected to. "Your brothers said you might be bringing someone to dinner."

"They're wrong. It's just me." He'd spent time with—okay, slept with—two other women since Ali, but they were mediocre at best. Not one rocked his world, but then again, he wasn't looking for permanent, was he?

His other sister, Tyler's twin Lexi, came to squeeze Sean around the shoulders. He hadn't seen her in too many days and couldn't help but notice the gleam in her eyes. He let out a groan and held Lexi away from him.

"Please tell me you don't have a new boyfriend."

She gave him a small, angelic smile she only whipped out when she needed to quiet her brothers' growls, but fact was that Lexi had terrible taste in men. Her last boyfriend had attempted to clean out her bank account, and since Lexi had suffered from a lack of oxygen during her birth and, consequently, a lack of talent for numbers, she hadn't realized until too late.

But Sean had personally overseen the mission to hunt down the boyfriend and teach him a lesson, with the help of Chaz, Dylan and Roades.

Colonel Jackson's words echoed in his head... *You're damn good at strategy, Knight.*

"Sean, leave your sister alone and go rescue those steaks," *Maman* said.

Shooting Lexi a pointed look that said he wasn't done with this, he went onto the deck. It wrapped the cabin on two sides and the waters

25

of the Louisiana swamps glittered in the sunlight. He dragged in a deep breath of the familiar scents of Spanish moss and bracken—and charring beef.

"Let me in there." He shouldered his way to the grill, and Tyler passed him the tongs.

"You're welcome to it, bro. Have fun."

At the end of the dock, his three brothers were kicked back with beers. Dahlia sat on Ben's knee, sipping a wine cooler. And their *pére* was gazing out over the bayou while talking with his brothers.

Sean got the steaks off the grill and checked them. None of the Knights liked their meat mooing at them and preferred them cooked medium, but these were blackened on the outside and definitely done more than they liked.

His ears pricked up on the conversation at the other end of the deck.

"Jackson Hole. Your *maman* has always wanted to go there," their father said.

"Does she know?" Dahlia asked, a smile on her pretty face.

Their father shook his head, his own smile in place. "Gonna surprise her after supper. Think she'll take to a getaway for our anniversary?"

Ben snorted. "If I know *Maman,* she won't want to leave her hellion daughters to their own devices, but they're old enough to do for themselves."

"I heard that." Tyler strode over to clap Ben on the ear, sending Dahlia into giggles. "Lexi and I can manage ourselves, thank you very much. We aren't kids anymore."

Looking at his tall, curvy sister wearing cutoffs that would rock the worlds of too many men, Sean would agree.

He waved the tongs at his family. "I agree—the girls will be fine. Whatever goes down with their love lives, I'm out of it. Unless some kind of heist is involved, and then I've got enough zip-ties and toolbox space to handle the problem."

His brothers all stared at him and Tyler shook her head. "Should we be hearing this, Sean? I thought your jobs are confidential."

He threw her a wink and carried the platter to the table. He barely set it down when a phone buzzed—a sound that was foreign out here without cell towers or electric.

Sean's gaze locked on Ben. Dahlia leaped off his lap as if that buzz had been a gigantic wasp stinging her in the backside. Ben withdrew the satellite phone from his back pocket, his stare locked on his fiancée as he answered.

"Knight." He listened for a second and then jammed his fingers through his too-long, not remotely military regulation hair. "Fuck. Now?"

Chaz, Dylan and Roades stood, at the ready. Sean's stomach growled at the scent of steaks, which he'd probably be missing out on if the look on Ben's face was anything to go by.

"Fine. We're leaving now." Ben tossed a look at each of the Knight Ops team.

"Oh no. You'll miss *Pere's* announcement to *Maman*," Tyler said faintly.

Ben pocketed the phone. "We gotta roll," he said to the team before reaching for Dahlia. He cradled her face in his hands and said something to her softly that made Sean turn away.

Sean was first to embrace his father and Tyler. Then he strode back inside the cabin to kiss his mother and Lexi. The worst thing about these missions was the leave-taking and seeing the looks on all of his loved ones' faces made him question whether he ever wanted a wife and family of his own. His safe return was never guaranteed.

Maman ran onto the deck, tendrils of her graying dark hair loose from her ponytail. "Now? You boys didn't get to eat!"

"I'm sorry, *Maman*." Ben kissed her cheek.

Chaz picked up a steak between two fingers and took a bite. Chewing, he came forward to pull Tyler's hair. "It's burnt but you can practice while our parents are away."

"What? Away! What are you talking about, Chaz Knight?" *Maman* whirled to look at her husband, who was wearing a Kiss the Cook apron, even though he wasn't cooking, as far as Sean could see.

Their father cleared his throat. "Guess it has to be a rushed announcement. I know you've always wanted to go to Jackson Hole, *cher*, and we'll be going next week for our anniversary."

"Oh my!" She flew into his arms, and Sean was grateful for the happy moment to carry with the four of them as they left the family for God-knew-what destination.

Within minutes, they'd used the pirogue to cross the bayou and were back on dry land. They didn't have the Knight Ops SUV so the only option was Dylan's compact car.

"How the fuck do you fit in this thing?" Sean asked as he smacked his head when ducking under the doorframe to get in the back seat.

Dylan grinned. "I have enough leg room." His seat was pushed the whole way back, leaving Sean's knees pinned to his chest.

The ride from the cabin seemed to drag on. Ben could only tell them they had a security breach and major crisis, but that he didn't know much else. And that Colonel Jackson hadn't even been the one to call—it had been an Air Force general.

"Tell me we're not picking up a flyboy on top of our squid," Chaz said, referring to Rocko, their only team member who wasn't a Knight and also happened to be Navy.

"I don't know," Ben said, staring out the windshield, lost in his own thoughts. Sean exchanged a look with his brothers. He couldn't help but feel his big brother's soul was back on that dock with the woman he loved.

* * * * *

"This is Air Force shit. Why is this our problem?" Sean's question hung in the air of the conference room, where they were seated waiting to hear all the details of the shit-storm that was about to hit them.

Ben shot him a look. "Because we're closer. Barksdale Air Force base is practically in our back yard."

Chaz smacked the top of the table with a palm. "Damn!"

Everyone directed their attention to his random outburst.

30

"I had a date tomorrow."

"You mean booty call." Dylan smirked.

"It's not a booty call if I bring takeout, dickhead."

"Oh, forgive me. Then it's dinner and a fuck. Does that constitute a date in your mind?" Dylan arched a brow.

Chaz gave him a flat stare. Each of the Knights were damn good at giving intimidating looks, but Chaz could make a man's balls shrivel almost more than Ben could. "We're keeping it on the down-low."

"Does that mean she's married?"

"I don't cheat, you asshole. We just can't let anything get out. Because of her position."

"Missionary," Rocko and Roades said at the same time, and then bumped knuckles.

Sean grinned but his mind was working over the puzzle. Chaz was tossing breadcrumbs, and nobody was picking them up.

"It's the DEA agent, isn't it? The one that we handed those pirates over to." One of their first missions had been to stop a huge drug shipment, along with a known terrorist about to step onto US soil. Chaz had eyed the curvy DEA agent who came to interfere, but Sean hadn't thought of her again.

From the narrowing of Chaz's eyes, Sean had hit the bulls-eye.

"Are you kidding me?" Ben scrubbed a hand over his face. "When do you guys get all this time to fuck? We've had all of five hours of leave since Knight Ops formed, I swear."

Sean leveled his gaze at him. "And still you manage to get a round or three in every day with Dahlia."

Ben began to respond but was cut off by Colonel Jackson entering, along with an Air Force general behind him. The Knight Ops team stood at attention, and Jackson waved a hand for them to be seated once more.

The man sat and spoke in his usual straightforward manner. "I take it you men have heard."

Ben nodded. "Warheads being transported from California to Barksdale. Three missing."

Jesus, three? Sean had assumed there was only one, but their stakes had just been raised.

"That's right. An extreme oversight that has some heads rolling as we speak." The general nodded at Ben. "I'm General Gear. Good to see you, men. And thank you for coming."

Sean felt that familiar tingle of excitement burning at the base of his spine. The sensation urged him not to just move toward the danger but to run at it with a deadly stealth and precision that never failed him. He shifted in his seat, eager to get up and move.

He listened to more of the story of how the warheads had been misplaced. Then General Gear added, "If we find these warheads were mistakenly loaded onto another bomber headed for Barksdale instead of in the wind like we believe, someone's ass is on the line. But we're going to operate as if that isn't the case and there are, in fact, three live ones on the ground."

"What do we need to do?" Ben asked.

Under his breath, Sean couldn't help but say, "Damn fly boys keep making a fucking mess to clean up."

Ben slanted him a look.

"You just want your own team," Chaz said.

Damn. Bringing up the DEA agent had backfired on Sean.

Everyone straightened, and Ben riveted Sean in his gaze. "What's this?"

Sean avoided Colonel Jackson's eyes. "I'm all in Knight Ops. But someday, I'd like to be something besides second in command."

"This is something to discuss in your leisure time, boys, and you don't have that right now. We need you to move as swiftly as possible," Jackson said.

"You need us to get you out of the jam before Americans learn the truth." Ben's words rang through the conference room as he spoke what was on everyone else's minds. "I can't believe that for the second time in a decade, the Air Force has lost a warhead."

General Gear eyed Ben with a deadly blank stare. He wasn't about to be spoken to that way, especially by a punk Marine turned OFFSUS.

A heartbeat passed and then Ben pushed out a sigh, composing himself once more. "Let me state these facts and correct me if I'm wrong. Before transport, the military was supposed to disarm eight warheads, but three slipped by inspection." He let this statement hang in the air, accusing the men involved not of incompetence but of possible treason. "Then en route to Barksdale, they were hijacked and are believed to be floating around the South somewhere."

"And we have about five minutes to find them before some redneck comes up with a scheme to take over the country," Sean said.

Colonel Jackson's gaze shot to him and then back to the general. "That sums it up, Knight. Question is, how are you boys going to find them?"

The group around the table sat dead still in various poses of contemplation. Dylan had his fingers to his temples and Chaz had rocked back in his chair to look at the ceiling. Roades only had his head cocked, staring without pause at the general as if the man had personally set out to ruin their fun at the cabin. And Rocko was his usual relaxed self, his ankle hitched over his knee and one arm stretched to the back of the empty seat next to him.

Ben looked like a warhead himself, all bottled up and about to blow. Sean couldn't blame him—leaving his girl for this kind of fuck-up that could have—*should* have—been avoided would piss anybody off.

"You say there's a buzz about it?" Sean asked.

The seven-star Air Force General nodded. "Some messages we believe to be related have recently been intercepted and we've got our best code cracker on the job. But she needs help."

Jackson turned his head to pierce Dylan in his gaze. "That's where you come in, Dylan."

He straightened. "I'll start now."

"I'll take you there in a minute. One more thing."

They all tensed. In this business, the other shoe *always* dropped. And it was never good.

"That Russian spy you had in your clutches a few days ago. He never made it to DC."

Sean reeled back in his seat. "Tell me you're fucking kidding me." He took back his comment about a redneck and replaced it with some Russian terrorist.

Jackson shook his head. "Something happened between the transport van and jet. Believe me, there are some military police in a world of shit right now for this little oversight. But I'll just put it out there that the Russian might have been in the South waiting for these warheads to show up."

"And now he's loose and so are the warheads," Ben concluded in an isn't-that-fabulous voice.

Jackson nodded. "Dylan, come with me. The rest of you have some planning to do. Use the room as long as you'd like."

The general stood and left with Jackson and Dylan on his tail. Sean glanced at his team. "Can you believe that shit? Letting that Russian go after the trouble we went through to capture him?"

"You're just pissed about wasting all those zip-ties on the man," Chaz quipped. His banter fell flat as the situation too heavy.

Ben got up and paced to the wall of tall windows overlooking the parking lot and beyond that, the coast.

Sean's mind worked over their course of action. What they really needed was a solid lead on locating the warheads or the spy. Without those, they were more or less wandering the South looking for a fox in a hole. And there were too many holes to look into and far too little time.

Pushing back his chair, Sean stood. Everyone stared at him. "I'm going with Dylan and see if I can at least get enough intel to find a starting point."

Ben turned from the window. "You'd better move it. They're crossing the parking lot right now."

Sean took off in a jog, navigating the corridors and pushing past the guards to get outside. He called out, and Jackson and Dylan stopped before getting into a black car. Sean caught up. "I'm going along to carry back any information that will help in the planning."

Jackson gave a sharp nod and opened the back door to climb in. Dylan and Sean exchanged a look and then Dylan climbed into the spacious back seat and Sean took shotgun with the driver. In minutes, he became aware that they didn't have the code analyst set up in an obvious part of the city. New Orleans had many richly cultural areas, and they were headed into voodoo and black magic territory. Typical undercover operation.

When they arrived at an old storefront, Sean suppressed a snort. Yup, he'd guessed it. The place looked to have been vacant since Hurricane Katrina.

The driver stopped along the curb and they all got out. Without waiting, Sean went inside the building and stopped, looking at the dust fallen on glass display cabinets and a circa-1990s cash register.

Someone came out of the back room, and Sean straightened, hand flying to his sidearm, the heel of his hand on the grip as he stared down the man who stood slightly taller than him.

Dressed in cargo pants and a T-shirt, the man could be military or just some wannabe. They eyed each other, and the guy took a step closer. Sean's fingers flexed on his weapon.

The man snorted. "Shoulda figured you'd be a dumbass, Knight. I'm not going to attack you. At ease."

Sean didn't budge, searching the guy's clothing for sign of rank, but there was no indication this guy could order him around. "Who the hell are you?"

"Jeeezus," the guy drawled as Jackson and Dylan entered behind Sean. "What did you bring me to work with, Colonel?"

"Hawk, meet the Knights, Sean and Dylan. Your charge will be working with Dylan here."

His charge?

"Hawk, as in Bo Hawkeye?" Sean asked.

The guy raised a thick brow at him. Sean's first impression was extreme dislike. He'd met some cocky motherfuckers in his day, but Hawk seemed to be outranking all of them in asshole factor.

They stood staring at each other like a couple of alley cats fighting over a food scrap, which was dumb because there was nothing to measure their dicks over.

Sean forced his hand away from his side and straightened his body into a non-combative stance. Whether or not he succeeded was anybody's guess.

"I'm with Dylan. I need to carry intel back to my team."

Hawk's nostrils flared slightly, but he didn't look away. Whatever the hell the guy's problem was, it couldn't be with him. Sean had never been in the same room with Hawk before, and he didn't give a fuck if he did offend him—he had a job to do.

When Sean stepped up to the guy, his chest inches away from Hawk's, he felt a ripple run across his skin that was pure adrenaline. After a long second, Hawk stepped aside, allowing him to pass into the room where Dylan had gone.

As he entered the cramped back room, his gaze flitted over cardboard boxes and work surfaces to one small desk in the corner where Dylan was seated. Next to him was a woman, her face partially hidden by the huge high-tech monitor she sat behind.

The analyst was female?

He stepped farther into the room, and the woman tipped her head up to peer over the monitor at him. Sean's chest constricted as his stare clashed with the warmest, biggest brown eyes he'd ever seen.

An odd spark struck his solar plexus and zipped through his entire body. Like being struck by a lightning bolt. What the hell was that?

He twitched his fingers into fists.

Dylan was completely engrossed in what was on the screen, oblivious to the moment that passed between Sean and this... this goddess? Code cracker. Special operative.

And Hawk was in charge of her? Jackson had said that, hadn't he?

The low voices of Jackson and Hawk in the other room rose and fell. For all Sean knew, they were comparing recipes, and he sure as hell hoped so. It would give him more time to get closer to the beauty seated next to his brother.

His very lucky brother, who was about to be overthrown.

He moved forward, circling a table that might have been a place to fold clothing items or roll out dough when this business was in operation. He had no idea what this shop had once been, but for the moment it was HQ.

The woman came more into view, the sight of her delivering another hit to the chest as he took in her sleek dark hair, the ends just below her collarbones. She appeared to be as fit as a Marine, with sharp shoulders and trim arms in a simple navy top. She wore no jewelry and no dog tags. But why would she if she was working for OFFSUS or some other government operation?

His lungs were burning, and he realized he wasn't breathing. He sucked in a breath and came to stand next to the desk. The beauty looked up at him, eyes wary but carrying a hint of amusement.

Her skin, café au lait with a dash of cream, had a richness he burned to see under the glow of candlelight. Or moonlight in the bayou. The vision of naked limbs and those plump dark pink lips of hers had his cock stirring.

Jesus, voodoo and black magic indeed. What the hell was this woman doing to him?

"I'm Knight." He stopped as that glimmer in her eyes brightened. She was laughing at him inside. And he was acting like a fool, as if he'd never met a woman in his life, let alone taken many to his bed. "Sean Knight."

"Nice to meet you." She didn't offer her name or her hand, and he didn't know which bothered him more. He needed her name—but he *wanted* to touch her skin, to make that contact that always bound humans together.

Had she shaken Dylan's hand? He slid his gaze to his brother, who was so engrossed he didn't even look up. His geek side was showing, but he let that flag fly with pride.

She tilted her head to the side, revealing two tiny silver studs in her earlobe. The daintiest, most feminine accessories Sean had ever seen. His fingertip tingled to reach out and stroke his finger across her lobe, but he couldn't touch her—not because he was a stranger but because he'd surely break such a creature.

"And your name is?" he prompted.

Dylan lifted his eyes from the screen and stared at Sean. Damn, was it that obvious that he was acting oddly?

"This is Special Operative Elise Dupré. She's been working for twenty hours straight on this message, and she's so close to having part of it stripped down." Dylan's voice rang with admiration.

No. That couldn't happen. Dylan was not working with this woman.

Elise.

Also, Sean didn't want to hear the words *stripped down* associated with Elise or coming from Dylan's mouth ever again.

He grabbed a metal folding chair and flipped it open, settling it next to the woman. Beside her, he looked like a mountain. She was smaller than he'd guessed, and he dwarfed her. A protective instinct rose up, unbidden.

It's my duty to protect anything more vulnerable than I am. I'm here to protect and serve.

God, could he serve her. Seating her on his face, her honey-brown thighs clasping his ears as he—

"This." Elise pointed to the screen, and Dylan followed her finger. Sean had no idea what they were seeing in the simple words. But he wasn't leaving his brother alone with Elise. The team could fill him in on the

43

operation later, because he was staying right here.

Dylan reached for the keyboard. "May I?"

Dammit, had they just exchanged a smile? No. Absolutely not.

Elise pushed the keyboard in his direction and Dylan tapped out some letters that at first glance, appeared to be scrambling the existing words. But he hit another key and a few letters were suddenly in bold type and spelling out something completely different.

"Kentucky? Fucking Kentucky," Sean growled.

Elise looked at him, eyes wide.

Feeling like a barbarian, he offered her a smile that felt utterly foreign on his face. Judging by the look on Dylan's, it appeared as weird as it felt.

"We've spent a lot of time in Kentucky recently," Sean said by way of explanation.

"Ah." The sound she uttered was so feminine, so fucking close to the sound she'd make in Sean's bed, that his jeans grew tight in the crotch.

"Do you believe the warheads are somewhere in Kentucky?"

She gave a light shake of her head that sent her hair brushing across those delicious collarbones. If Sean got fully hard while seated on this folding chair, his fly was going to burst.

Dylan and Elise began talking fast, skipping over parts that Sean didn't understand, leaving him to fill in the blanks as if they were speaking a foreign language and he was only comprehending every third word.

Elise raised her hands and started fluttering her fingers in the air, seeming to outline things nobody could see but he assumed her brilliant mind made perfect sense of.

Dammit, this woman was intriguing, alluring, smart and giving off the appeal of a voodoo priestess oozing sex and magic. Looking at her, he wouldn't doubt she had someone just like that in her family tree.

And Dylan was going to work with her? No.

"Dylan, can I speak with you alone?" His words came out harsh, stopping their chatter dead.

They both stared at him. Dylan gave a single nod and then looked to Elise. She went back to the screen as Sean stood and walked out of the room. He had to make something clear, and he was damn well pulling rank.

It would take a crash-course in codes and data, but Sean was a quick study with languages, and this couldn't be much different, right? He was more than ready. He just had to get his brother out of the way.

Dylan was stepping aside so Sean could take his place.

Chapter Three

Elise looked on as Dylan followed Sean out of the room. And then walked right back in. They stood in the corner, backs to her and heads together, speaking in low tones she couldn't make out but giving her one hell of a view.

Two chiseled bodies, the sets of their shoulders so similar they could be twins. Sean's hair was a hint darker, or that could just be the crappy overhead lighting in this dump Bo had set her up in.

Why she couldn't analyze the messages from the comfort of her own apartment, she had no clue, but as soon as he'd learned she would have the help of Dylan Knight, Bo had whisked her here.

At least he'd given her the biggest, best monitor on the market to work with.

She wasn't letting these guys step in and steal her work out from under her. This was far too exciting, and she wasn't about to hand it over to the Knight brothers.

She chewed at her lower lip as she tried to focus on the work and failed. It was impossible not to wonder what the brothers were discussing in such heated whispers, especially given her guess that they were taking over.

Dylan suddenly straightened with a jerk and Sean turned to give Elise a smile.

Oh no. She was working with one of *those* guys. The charm-your-panties-off playboy types. That was the last thing she needed. What she required to do her job, and essentially save Americans, was an intelligent, focused assistant. Instead, she was getting Tweedle Dee and Tweedle Dum.

She returned his stare but not his smile. "Look, I don't give a damn what your credentials are. You're not pushing me out of this and taking over."

Sean stared at her. "Why would you think we're taking over?"

She stood and planted her hands on her hips. "This is my area of specialty, and I'm more qualified for it than two guys who've spent their days taking orders."

Ouch. She wasn't normally such a bitch, but she was an angry momma bear, determined to protect this mission and see it through to the end.

Sean shook his head. "We're not here to take over."

"Well, whatever your problem is, it is no importance compared to this." She waved at the screen and the thousands of codes to be broken—her first priority, not babysitting two overgrown, though hot, special ops guys.

Dylan turned to face her too, his face red with what she took as anger. "Elise, Sean's going to be working with us."

Her gaze shifted to the other brother. A resigned sigh left her. "Fine. Three sets of eyes are better than one."

She returned to her work, becoming engrossed in seconds. When the men took their seats flanking her, she hardly noticed until a whiff of aftershave wiggled into her psyche. She pointed at two letters, and Dylan nodded.

"What are you seeing?" Sean asked.

She glanced at him from the corner of her eye. Did he really have no clue what he was doing? *Please tell me this isn't your first rodeo.*

When she didn't answer, Dylan spoke. "The letter B is standing in for the fourth letter of the alphabet, D."

They continued on. When Dylan broke another between two letters, Elise's excitement bubbled. Together they could do this. They couldn't fail. Sean picked out a few of the words as well, and within a short time, they had a sentence.

It wasn't until they decoded the second sentence in the passage when she noticed something going on between the brothers. When Dylan would try to speak, Sean would jump in. Was this some sibling rivalry or the typical pissing match she'd seen among Marines since joining up years ago?

She lowered her eyes and covertly glanced at each man. Dylan seemed to be concentrating on the work, and Sean's gaze wandered from the words to her fingers on the keys. Or maybe he wanted to take over the keyboard.

Fine, let the jerk have something to do besides sit there making her nervous. She shoved it his way. "You're welcome to it."

He twisted his lips and then released them so fast that she might have imagined the small quirk of his lips. Bad boys like Sean Knight would make that expression in their sleep — it was nothing to do with her.

Dylan recited a few letters, which Sean tapped in with precision, his long, tanned fingers spanning across the keys. With Sean doing that part of her job, Elise had laser focus on her work. She had no idea of the shadows falling across the room until a step in the doorway made her look up.

Bo cocked a brow at her as if to say, Everything okay?

She gave the faintest of nods.

Bo cleared his throat. "I assume you're working through the night, but Elise needs to sleep. She's been up for twenty-nine hours."

Sean's head whipped up and the muscle of his thigh closest to her tensed. She guessed that if she touched the denim-covered muscle that it would be the same makeup as concrete. Confusion made her look between her ex-husband and the man she'd just met.

A gasp of understanding hit her lips. They must be acquainted, and some dislike was making them circle each other like angry dogs. Their teeth might not be bared, but she sensed it nonetheless.

Either way, she didn't have time for it. "I'll crash here if I need to. Go on home, Bo."

Sean made a rough noise that drew all of their attention to him. He cleared his throat to cover the moment, but he definitely didn't have something caught there. What the hell had been foisted on her? Dylan was fine — intelligent, professional. Why did he have to drag his brother into this?

She looked to Bo again. Lines of fatigue ran from his eyes to the corners of his mouth. If anyone needed to hit the pillow, it was him.

She raised her chin, indicating he should go. He nodded and turned to leave.

As soon as Bo was out of the space, Sean stood and stretched. His big frame shaking as joints popped.

She gave him the side-eye. Why was a stretch so damn hot? It shouldn't be.

Dylan stood too and walked over to part a grubby blind with his fingers and look out. This block of the city was pretty desolate, and she doubted even a stray cat wandered the streets.

"I think takeout is out of the question. Nobody's going to deliver back here."

"We don't need takeout. There's a fridge in the other room packed with drinks and food, as well as a microwave." Her statement made both men gawk at her.

"Why didn't you say something? I've been sitting here with cotton-mouth for hours." Sean strode into the other room and returned with two bottled waters and two sub sandwiches cupped in one large hand.

He set these before her.

"Thank you."

"Can't have you dropping over from hunger or fatigue. Why don't you eat and then sleep? I saw a padded booth out there that would serve as a pallet."

She didn't like the way his concern flowed so easily from his lips—she got enough of that from Bo, and there was only room for one Bo in her life. She cracked open the water and downed half of it while Sean watched her, sipping at his own drink.

Dylan made a grunting noise that had them both turn to eye him. He glanced from the window. "What if the letter U isn't a factor at all?"

Elise set down her bottle and leaned forward to peer at the screen. Her mind worked furiously over Dylan's statement, but the low growl emitted from Sean had her head snapping.

The man stared at a point across the room and at nothing in particular, the sub and drink forgotten in his hands. His eyelids fluttered. "It's an equation."

She shot to her feet, torn between getting this straight in her mind and continuing with their breakthrough. "Wait. You're new to this game, so how are you figuring this out?"

"Sean's a quick study," Dylan said.

Sean spouted an equation that left her reeling. "Holy shit," she whispered. "That's the burn rate. Mass ratio, delta v and exhaust velocity."

He nodded slowly, as if in a trance.

"Jesus, Dylan. Is your brother some kind of savant or something? He looks like he's going to drop to the floor and have a seizure. Or maybe he's channeling the man who wrote the code." She stared at Sean, who hadn't moved a muscle.

Dylan drifted to the big table serving as a desk and leaned over to look at the screen. He grunted. "I'd say he's right."

Stunned, she watched Sean return to normal and take a bite off the sub sandwich so big it seemed his jaws could hardly manage to chew it. But he gnawed it down to nothing and then swallowed, flashing her a grin.

What the hell? She'd never seen anyone operate like this man. It was hard not to be impressed, but she knew better than to show it. She'd lived with a cocky Marine for six months, after all. Heaping praise on Bo had been like tossing dry leaves on a raging fire. It doubled, tripled the man's ego.

But damn, he was good. She shook her head, unable to stop her smile from stretching her lips. Maybe for the next few days, there was room in her life for another man like her ex. But for now, she was dead on her feet, swaying with fatigue, her mind already clouding and her eyelids drawing downward as if weighted.

"I'm going to crash," she muttered, heading to the front room. As she fell into the booth, she felt something warm and soft cloak her shoulders. Cracking an eye, she saw Sean hovering over her.

"It's just my coat to keep you warm. I'll see what they can do about setting us up in a nice hotel so you can at least have a bed next time. Sleep, *cher*."

Her eyes slammed shut but her mind worked on and on—not over the codes or the equation Sean had spouted, but over the strange look on his face as he stood over her, covering her in his coat.

* * * * *

Sean leaned back in his seat, stretching the sore and stiff muscles of his spine after long hours hunched over the table, staring at a screen. Numbers and letters floated before his eyes, along with some spots that told him he was too tired to go on. He needed to break.

"This is a bullshit place. Did Hawk set Elise up here? If so, he must be into torture. No comforts, no amenities. She's out there sleeping in a fucking old booth on ripped vinyl." He waved toward the front of the building where Elise slept. He'd been checking on her hourly. So far, she'd been dead to the world for four hours. In that time, he and Dylan had uncovered so much more.

They were looking at more international involvement than they'd originally thought.

Dylan stared at him after his outburst but only gave a shake of his head. "I think this place is used often by OFFSUS. It's ideal for undercover operations really—no foot traffic, no nosy people peeking in the windows."

"It's a bad part of town that no woman should be traveling to alone."

Dylan leveled his gaze at him. "It's likely that Hawk brought Elise here. She wasn't alone. Besides, you know she's a decorated Marine, right?"

"Yeah."

"But do you know took care of that KKK Grand Wizard up in Tulsa?"

Sean's brows shot up. "That was her?"

Dylan nodded.

"Holy shit." Stories got stretched but the bottom line was that Elise had crept into a white supremacist church and gotten several teams on the scene to confiscate all the weapons there. She'd done her job and could have walked out, but then she'd set eyes on the Grand Wizard and taken matters into her own hands.

Sean blew out a whistle. Brains and skill— sexy as hell.

Dylan nodded.

"What do you know about her and Hawk?" he asked.

For hours he'd been trying to puzzle out the relationship or the odd vibes he'd gotten from Hawk and Elise when they were in the same room, and he couldn't. If they were lovers, he had no idea what Elise saw in that arrogant bastard.

"No more than you. You look like hell and if you don't sleep, you'll be no good to any of us. Get up and walk around or go find a corner to sleep in."

What he wanted to do was crawl into that booth with Elise, curl around her body and keep her warm and safe.

At that moment, she appeared in the doorway. Straight hair slightly mussed and a vinyl imprint on her cheek but still stunning. Sean's nuts could attest to just how hot she looked.

What he wouldn't do to rouse her from sleep and slide into her tight little body...

"What'd I miss, boys?" She strode across the room and looked between them.

"There's a lot of information." Dylan pointed at the monitor.

Sean stood to allow Elise to pass to her chair in the middle. She still smelled of a sweet vanilla musk, which shocked his senses. In fact, the scent seemed to be more intense after sleep.

She sank to the seat and her jaw dropped. "Holy shit."

Sean and Dylan nodded.

"Did you send this on yet? Hawk will need to see it — to get it to the right people." She pivoted to look into Sean's eyes. For a second, he was blinded by her direct stare, and all he could think about were steamy nights with entangled limbs and soft sighs. The state of the country's security had flown right out of his head.

"I haven't forwarded it yet. I thought you should see it," Dylan said.

She spun back to the screen, checking their work like some special ops schoolteacher. What a sexy thought.

"But... this looks off. Are you sure this is correct? It's a place, so we need to ensure it's correct and I'm not sure..."

Sean and Dylan leaned in to stare at the grouping of words she was speaking of. Sean blinked to clear his vision, his eyes bleary, and he smacked a hand off the desk. "Dammit, it's wrong and that's my fault."

He jerked to his feet and paced to the window that looked out on... well, nothing. It was pitch-black outside, and the city didn't seem to bother with streetlights here. He couldn't even see a glimmer of the moon.

Silence descended on the room. For a moment, Dylan and Elise didn't speak. Probably secretly laughing behind his back at his fuck-up, a mistake that could have sent the Knight Ops in the wrong direction in search of the warheads.

He slammed the heel of his hand off the window frame. "Fuck!"

Dylan was by far the better man for this operation, and Elise was an expert as well. Sean was just in the way. So why couldn't he bring himself to walk away and join the rest of his team?

A chair creaked as someone got up. He didn't turn.

A second later, warmth washed over his skin, and he knew it wasn't Dylan coming to speak with him. He glanced down at Elise. Christ, the top of her head only reached his shoulder. She carried herself in that tall, proud way only a Marine could and if he had any doubt as to how she'd ended up in this position, he didn't now.

"Sean, it's an easy error to make. The reversal of two letters."

"Knights don't fuck up." He sent Dylan a look and got a nod of agreement. His brother wasn't going to sugarcoat it and tell him it was okay that he'd made such a monumental mistake.

"Everyone fucks up. It's why there are more than one of us on this job. Because we can catch the errors before they get too far."

"She's right," Dylan added with a yawn. "Besides, you've only been doing this for what — eight hours? You're practically just learning to crawl."

Fucking Dylan. Leave it to him to put things in perspective and expose his soft spots all in one fucking sentence.

"Get some sleep, Sean," Dylan said.

"The booth's not half bad," Elise said, her brows stitched with concern, or maybe a grimace at the thought of sleeping in that uncomfortable place.

"I'm getting Jackson on the phone and finding us better accommodations. This is bullshit. And I can't take the booth — my shoulders won't even fit to lie down."

Elise stood so close, her heady scent overwhelmed him. He was tired and his ego was slightly bruised. All he wanted was a juicy steak, a beer and a long, slow fuck followed by a solid night's sleep where he didn't have to worry about warheads in the hands of people

60

who could destroy what their country had worked hundreds of years to build.

He sucked in a deep breath, filling his head with Elise's perfume and in turn, his cock twitched to semi-hardness. When she met his gaze, his stomach dipped like he'd just stepped off a cliff. It almost immediately righted itself, but a trail of heat burned low in his groin.

Her lips parted, and he watched her draw her lower one in to nibble at the plump flesh.

Hell, now he was fully hard. A throb began.

He searched her eyes for a long minute, attached by some invisible thread, unable to look away.

She broke the connection first, twisting her head aside and looking back toward Dylan. "Stretch out on the floor then. Just get some sleep. And don't worry about the error—we work as a team, and it doesn't just fall on your shoulders." She looked up at him again, gaze locked on his left shoulder and slowly traveling to the right as if measuring them with her eyes.

His cock throbbed harder. He had to get out of here, away from her, before he acted on this crazy lust pounding his system. She wouldn't appreciate any move he might make, and he wasn't going to embarrass himself further.

"Maybe I should carry this intel back to Jackson myself," he said.

"No, Bo's coming back for it. He doesn't trust just anyone."

A growl rose unbidden in Sean's throat. It was bad enough she called Hawk "Bo," but it sounded as if she looked forward to his return.

"Fine, I'll go close my eyes for a bit. They're blurry anyway." He avoided Elise's stare as he walked out of the room. In the front, he glanced at the booth. Absolutely out of the question. If he managed to squeeze between the table and the seat back, he'd need the Jaws of Life to free him.

He spotted his jacket Elise had used as a blanket folded neatly and draped over the back of the booth. His chest tightened as he picked it up and brought it to his nose. Yep, it smelled like her, and he wanted to roll in her scent.

The thought caught him off-guard. He'd never thought these things about another woman, nor had he ever imagined he would. He—

The door opened behind him, and he whirled, weapon drawn and trained on the one man he actually felt like shooting right now.

"Fuck off, Knight." Hawk closed the door and locked it again. "You leavin'?" He looked to the jacket in Sean's hands.

"Hell no." And he wasn't going to close his eyes now either, now that this asshole was here.

Hawk dismissed him and strode to the doorway. A "Hi, Bo," came from Elise, and Sean rushed to the door too, determined to catch some look on her face that might reveal what Hawk was to her.

But Elise hadn't looked up from the monitor. Dylan glanced at Sean but said nothing. At least his brother knew when to keep his mouth shut when necessary.

"What, no greeting, Elise?" Hawk moved forward and she finally gave him a smile.

Sean clenched his fingers in his jacket, mashing the cloth and wishing it was Hawk's balls.

"I did greet you. You don't get a parade in your honor as a way of hello."

He strolled to her side and rested his hands on her shoulders, lightly kneading them. A pleasured sigh left her as she dropped back into touch. "That feels divine. I'm so knotted up."

"But you got some sleep. I can tell."

Fuck, he could *tell*? That must mean he'd seen her sleep deprived as well as rested. Sean's growl made them all look up. Dylan wore a curl of a smile at the corner of his

63

mouth, and Sean wanted to punch it off his damn face.

Hawk went back to massaging Elise's shoulders. After another half a minute, he stopped and looked at the screen. "How much do you have for me?"

"About fifteen pages."

He straightened, his demeanor changing entirely from that easygoing friend of Elise's to commander. "That's all?"

She pushed to her feet, facing down the mountain of muscle. If Hawk laid one hand on her, Sean would end him. No hesitation. He and his brothers had enough skill to hide the body of a self-important OFFSUS agent in the swamps too.

Dylan made a noise of warning, but Sean continued to glare at Hawk as he accused Elise of slacking on the job.

Except he didn't have to—she was laying into the man with the sharp edge of her tongue. "Why don't you give it a go, you know-it-all man?"

"Fifteen pages is hardly worth carrying."

"It has some excellent intel. Things we—"

"Elise, it's not enough. Do you understand the pressure they're putting on me to give them the jump they need? I don't have time for this."

"Well, then give us some damn help. This isn't a few short love letters, Bo. It's a fucking bible worth of information to decipher, and it's by far one of the most complex...—"

"Lay off her," Sean said quietly.

Oh shit. That wasn't good. When he went quiet, shit went down and heads rolled.

Hawk spun to pierce him in his glare.

"She's been at it forty hours with just a few of rest."

Hawk lifted a brow, and Sean took a menacing step forward. If this was how it had to be, then he was prepared for hand-to-hand combat.

"If it's not fast enough for you, then do as Elise suggested and give us help. More teams and some fucking better accommodations, for Chrissakes."

Elise stared at Sean, wide-eyed. Then she raised a hand and rested it on Bo's forearm. "We have a world to save—getting it right is as important as getting the intel in time."

"Fine. Consider it done. I'll move you right now and get you the help you need." Hawk didn't look down at Elise as he spoke but gazed at Sean. "Your team's heading out."

Dylan and Sean exchanged looks. Would Dylan argue about who stayed and who joined the Knight Ops? Frankly, Dylan was the better

65

man for the job, but Sean couldn't walk away from this challenge.

Dylan nodded. "I'll go." He moved around the table and picked his way across the crowded space to reach Sean. He held up a hand, and Sean clasped it, squeezing.

"Take care, bro. Guts and glory," he recited what had been their motto the past few missions.

"Guts and glory." Dylan clapped him on the back with his free hand and then disappeared.

Sean faced Hawk once more. Elise stood next to him, no longer touching him. That was something to celebrate, at least. Sean needed something good to think about rather than the fact that he was abandoning his team—his *brothers*—to do a job he was unskilled at.

For what? So he could remain close to Elise?

But a thrum deep inside him told him he was doing the right thing. He folded his arms across his chest and stared back at Hawk. "Get those accommodations made. And make sure Elise has her own bed."

Chapter Four

When Bo had agreed to a new HQ, Elise had expected an abandoned office building or even a top floor of a hotel. But the man had commandeered an entire inn overlooking the coast and installed two other two-man teams so they could work around the clock.

And she had gotten her own bed, a private room decorated very similarly to her bedroom in her place. Upon opening the dresser drawers, she hadn't been surprised to find fresh clothing—jeans, T-shirts and cozy sweats as well as undergarments—all in her size. Having a metrosexual best friend ex-husband with enough power to pull strings was definitely a perk.

And Sean... She couldn't quit thinking about the way he'd stood up to Bo, who was known to be a bit of a ball-breaker, especially to any Marine ranked beneath him. But Sean had stood his ground and made demands of his own.

One of those demands had been for her comfort, and thinking about it gave her a small quivery feeling all over. She firmly put it out of her head for the dozenth time since arriving at the inn.

What had been the dining room of the place was now decked out with state of the art technology, and the four people working with them had nerded-out over the systems as much as Elise had. While Sean stood back watching with amusement on his handsome face, she and the others had talked over the system's features like PMS-ing women talked about chocolate.

It had taken all of twenty minutes before it became a battle of teams. Or battle of nerds, as Sean had called it. His lumping himself into that group made her smile even now. He wasn't the typical Brainiac she knew. No, he was more hands-on, trained for combat.

But she couldn't help but admire how quickly he'd caught on to deciphering the codes. That was sexy as hell, whether she wanted to admit it or not.

And she most certainly did not.

Elise dressed in a soft pullover top and jeans that hugged her perfectly. Bo was a much better shopper than she was—he knew what would flatter her shape, and she didn't mind giving the task up to him. When she stepped out of her room, Sean was waiting for her.

Leaning against the opposite wall of the hallway, his chiseled form looked entirely out of place against the floral wallpaper. He pulled away from the wall and offered her a crooked smile.

She went totally still. Staring at him. A dream flashed in her memory. It had been lost upon waking but that little half-smile had brought it to the surface, smacking her square in the face with the dream of her tracing her fingers over those well-shaped lips just before she leaned in and kissed him.

Hell no. She had to ditch the dream ASAP. She couldn't be recalling those slow kisses or the wet flip of his tongue against hers that her stupid mind had conjured in a state of total exhaustion. No, she was responsible and couldn't let him see what she was thinking.

Except he was staring at her closely with an amused crinkle at his eyes.

"Ready?" she asked breezily, striding past him down the corridor at a speed that had never been made for this coastal inn where vacationers lounged and found a slower pace in life.

She felt his hot gaze on her backside. Or she was imagining it. She had to be.

But she was a woman, and women had instincts. Sean Knight was checking out her ass, she was sure of it.

As they hit the dining room to relieve the other team, she recalled Bo's words as he'd given them the tour of their accommodations. *Access to the shore.*

Sean's response had been, "Good, I can train."

The urge to turn and look at him again, to see if his muscles were bulging from exercise and the veins snaking down his arms a result of hard work claimed her. She pivoted to look at him.

He smiled again, and she spun away. Dammit, what was with this guy? Bo had asked her the same before practically stalking out, leaving her wondering what the hell *his* problem was.

But Sean had voiced it. "What's with him? You hook up?"

She'd given a short, tense laugh. "He's my ex. No. Absolutely no hooking up."

Sean's face had been unreadable, a mask lowered over his normally expressive face.

She looked to him now. "Let's get to work."

The other team got up and passed the proverbial baton to Team Elise and Sean. The blonde woman looked exhausted, with slumping shoulders and rings under each eye.

70

She glanced between Elise and Sean. "You two don't look like the type to do this job."

Elise started. "What do you mean?"

"You're both too good-looking, too debonair. You're like a couple of international spies posing as a married couple."

"You've been up too long staring at numbers, Marissa." Elise laughed, but the sound was too sharp. Being lumped with Sean in the way Marissa had said was unnerving.

The pair left, and Sean and Elise took up their seats.

"International spies," Sean mused.

"Let's get to work. The clock is ticking and we're so close to having what we need." Her tone was more snappish than she intended, and he just stared at her. His direct gaze burying too deep inside her skin, making her feel restless in a way she never had before and couldn't understand.

Ignoring her partner and diving into her work was best—and essential to her sanity. She tried to focus on anything but how good he smelled as she began working the codes.

* * * * *

"Oh my God, why isn't this obvious to me?" Elise said for the third time. She had run her fingers through her hair, making it fluffier, more exotic looking. Even in the height of her frustration, she was sexy as hell.

Sean pushed out a sigh. "We've hit a wall, *cher.*"

She eyed him the way she had each time he used the Cajun endearment. He was growing to like her glares as much as her rare smiles.

"We aren't doing any good right now. We either skip this part and come back to it or let another team take over. Their minds are fresh. We've been at this seven hours," he said.

"No. No, I'm not walking away. It's right there—I can almost see it just out of reach. Why won't it come to me?"

He leaned closer. "Because you need a break. C'mon." He nudged her shoulder. "Get up. Let's go for a run."

"What?"

"You know, when you make your legs move to carry you faster across the ground?"

She compressed her lips, but he saw a flash of laughter in her eyes. "I can't go for a run now. I'm—"

"Not dressed for it. I agree. So go change into workout clothes and meet me out front." With that, he got up and walked out.

72

She sat there a long second, staring at the indecipherable words on the screen. She could continue to work and try to crack it or —

Sean was right — she *was* burnt out. Maybe a run would do her good.

She abandoned her post and waved to the next team seated in the lounge with a chessboard between them. "You're up," she said and went to her room to change.

Minutes later, she stepped outside to see Sean in shorts, running shoes and low socks. Nothing else.

She blinked at the sight of his chest, arms and shoulders on full display. Tattoos that hadn't been visible sneaked down his shoulder and a huge eagle with wings spread took up one pec, a part of him that seemed to fit like nothing else could. He'd probably come out of the womb looking like this.

The man was a damn powerhouse, that was sure. Tanned, chiseled, each dip and swell looking as if he'd spent time oiling himself up. She wouldn't put it past him — he *did* seem full of himself.

Hadn't she also thought that of Bo a few months after meeting him? They'd worked together closely, become a team. Then one day he'd kissed her, said they should make it a team in all ways and asked her to marry him. From the start, she'd known it was a bad decision. She and Bo just weren't cut out for that kind of relationship.

But Sean...

He was grinning at her as he lifted his knees to limber up. "Ready? You'd better stretch first. Don't want you pulling anything."

Ideas of him stretching out over her, tongues entangled, popped into her head.

She jerked into action, holding her knee to her chest and feeling a light pull along her thigh from sitting too long.

"You're in great shape." Sean's gaze wandered over her tank top and compression shorts.

"Thanks. So are you."

The grin was back, wider this time. Terrific—she'd fed his ego. Just what she needed.

After another few moves, he said, "Ready?"

"Sure."

"Can you keep up?" He took off in a jog that quickly became a sprint. Then Elise was laughing, legs and arms pumping as she gained on him. He was messing with the wrong woman—she was known for her speed.

He tossed her a grin, feet flying across the shore, and kicked it up a notch. His longer legs shot him forward, leaving her behind too many paces to recover. So she slowed to a natural pace and just enjoyed the feeling of heat in her unused muscles.

Sean realized she wasn't keeping up and circled back to her side. "Sorry. I have four brothers. But it's my younger sister who's really competitive. I can never run without making it into a competition."

They ran alongside each other for another couple steps. Then she took off, calling out, "I have brothers too!"

"Damn, woman!" His footsteps pounded behind her, but she had hit her stride and she could run for miles at this speed. She'd proved with Bo that just because he had longer legs didn't mean he could beat her. She planned to show Sean the same thing. He might be built for speed but she could go the distance.

After half a mile, his voice reached her. "Okay, you win!"

She slowed and let him catch up. Throwing a glance his way was a mistake, because the man was even hotter with sweat glistening on his chest.

She could get into some major trouble with a guy like Sean.

Especially since her radar was telling her to steer clear. He liked women, that was obvious, and he knew how to charm. But she wasn't interested in being one of his conquests. *Except one night would be fun.*

No. Absolutely not. She shushed her libido and focused on her breathing so she could hold a conversation.

"You're fast," he said.

"Thanks."

He held out his fist for her to bump her knuckles. Okay, this she could do—bros fist-bumped and the action would keep him firmly in the friend zone.

"How many brothers?" he asked.

"Two."

"Both military?"

"Yes."

"When did you join up?"

"2010." She wanted the attention off her. For some reason, she didn't want him to get too close. And did he wear that adorable smirk nonstop? He hadn't lost it since they'd gone outside the inn. She didn't want to admit that the quirk of his lips was growing on her and that she could trace the outline with her eyes closed.

That same quivery feeling inside her stomach made her increase her pace.

"What's the hurry? The operation is in good hands. We don't need to rush back."

Her mind snapped to their work. "I don't like leaving it unsolved."

He nodded. "I get it. We're trained to complete a job at all costs. But the longer we sat there, the more frustrated we got."

She chewed her lip. "You're right."

He leaned forward, putting his face in hers. "Wait—what did you just say?"

She slapped him aside, but he came right back, those hazel eyes full of mischief and his hair damp with perspiration. "Get out of my face, Knight."

"I didn't hear you clearly. Can you repeat what you just said?"

She cuffed him in the jaw, making him stumble right in her path. She slammed into him and they pitched forward, hitting the ground. The breath whooshed from her as she landed on top of his chest, which was like hitting a brick wall.

Her bare thighs were twisted at odd angles, the sole of his running shoe digging into her calf. She shifted, which only brought her hips flush against his.

His gaze met hers, forcing the last of her breath out of her. She stared down into his eyes, thinking of how the colors reflected the forest, when she came to her senses.

She pushed off, rolling in the dirt and coming up into a sitting position.

He got to his knees and reached for her. "Are you okay? I'm sorry—I shouldn't have been screwing off. Did you twist your ankle or anything?"

She panted. "I'm fine." Except she wasn't—her body was on fire after the barest touch of his.

Leaping to her feet, she brushed the grains of sand and dirt off her clothes. Sean stood with the swift move of a Marine at the ready. Oh, he was locked and loaded, all right. She'd felt every hard inch of him through his shorts.

How did a man even run with such a beast between his legs?

And why was he sporting it to begin with?

She burned to glance down at the front of his shorts but kept her gaze trained on her arms as she wiped away the dirt. Her concentration was crap, and she dropped her gaze.

Heat climbed her cheeks. Yeah, he was packing. Sweet mother, was he.

Reaching out, he used his knuckles to brush away some grains of sand from her cheekbone. "You sure you're okay? We can turn back."

"No, let's go on. I need the exercise to think."

The case was far from her mind, and what she needed to think on had nothing to do with codes. No, it was the way her body had reacted to falling on top of him.

* * * * *

Sean had been hard for most of the day. Okay, not just hard—aching. After watching Elise's shapely legs and ass and then her falling on top of him... well, he was only human.

And he was also lying to himself. He wanted her—had from the first time he laid eyes on her. He was finished with fooling himself. Also, his reason for being irritated with Hawk had to do with how much he desired Elise.

Even a cold shower after their run hadn't cut the need inside him. Now she was seated so close, smelling delicious and wearing a fitted T-shirt and sweatpants rolled down at the waist to bare her flat belly, and he was losing his fucking mind.

At least he'd thought he was losing his mind before he realized she wasn't wearing a bra and the cloth of her shirt molded to her small breasts and tight nipples. *Then* he was really losing it.

He ran a hand over his face for the third time, trying to wipe away the nonexistent drool. She was oblivious to his self-control issues as she stared at the screen for the second minute straight.

He was about to nudge her when she let out a gasp.

She slammed her hands onto the table and cried, "That's it!" She jumped up, as if she held too much energy to remain sitting. He gazed up at her, but that was worse—her soft breasts were hovering somewhere around his eyeballs, the centers beaded.

He couldn't take it anymore.

"What's it?" he grated out.

She blinked at him, a confused smile on her face. Then she shook her head. "I got it! I figured out how to crack this code!"

Her breasts jiggled in her excitement, which only caused more... *ahem*... excitement in him. His cock was bursting.

Taking a risk on his life, in case she decided to use her Marine training on him, he placed his hands on her hips and urged her back into the chair. His fingers flexed on her flesh, hard and soft at the same time. Christ,

80

what was he going to do now? It would take an explosion to peel his fingers off her.

For a dizzying moment, he considered tugging her down into his lap. Imagining the feel of her backside cradling his cock pulled a groan from him.

Up until this point, she'd been dead still, but now she stepped back. He gripped her hips again before he dropped his hands.

She took her seat next to him again, avoiding his gaze. "I… I know how to solve this now."

As she explained the process, he gawked at her. She talked with her hands, a flush coating her pretty face. He realized that for the first time ever, he was just as attracted to a woman's mind as he was her physical appearance.

The longer she talked, the more he stared until she stuttered to a stop and turned her dark eyes on him. "You don't think it's going to work?"

He shook his head. "I wasn't thinking that at all."

"Then what were you thinking? I'd like to hear your take."

He pushed out a breath, chest burning to blurt everything going on inside his head, from how much he admired her abilities, to his desire—no *need*—to suck her nipples until she moaned out his name.

She was staring at him expectantly. Fuck, what to say to her?

"I think that you're as brilliant as you are beautiful. Now let's get this cracked."

She blinked, her lips a small O of surprise, and then she redirected her attention to the screen. But her foot was tapping under the table, only causing her breasts to jiggle more.

Hell, it was going to be the longest afternoon of his life. A never-ending loop of torment.

Seconds later, she put fingers to keys and flew through several equations and cross-analyzation that had his head spinning.

"Look at this," she cried, excitement taking hold.

"Yes, it's an address? Jesus, it is. It's—"

"A street number," they said together.

"Oh my God, I can't believe it," she practically squealed.

He couldn't tear his gaze off her—she was so freakin' gorgeous.

She threw her palm up for a high-five, and he smacked his hand off hers, lightly closing his hand over her fingers for a brief second.

Her eyes flashed and he swore her breaths came faster. Was she feeling it too? This attraction was beyond anything he'd known before.

They grinned at each other, and something else passed between them, far more than a simple working relationship. The way she slid her gaze away told him she was uncomfortable with whatever emotions coursed through her when she looked at him. But he was far from uneasy about them. He wanted her.

For another twenty minutes, they worked away, filling in each other's sentences and running through more material than they and the previous teams had before. When the final message was deciphered, she leaped up, fist-punching the air at their success.

He couldn't hold back anymore. He got to his feet and closed his hands over her shoulders. Stunned, she tipped her head back to meet his gaze. Something broke in her eyes and she made a soft noise.

No more holding back. He was a man of action.

"*Cher*, I've been wanting to do this since the first moment I saw you." Leaning in, he moved around the chair to claim her sweet, plump lips.

* * * * *

Elise stilled in Sean's grasp, her heart pounding her ribcage like a trapped bird. His lips could not be on hers.

They most certainly *were* on hers.

He was kissing her.

And he tasted of pure male and a hint of the lemon water he'd taken a sip of a bit ago. The feel of any man's lips besides Bo's was completely foreign to her, and she was too stunned to do much more than stand there.

He wasn't forcing his tongue into her mouth or yanking her against his big, hard body, even though she ached for him to do so. He held her in place, the faintest brush of his lips across hers sending a thousand zaps to her nerve endings.

Most of them between her thighs.

A shiver ran through her, and he issued a guttural groan. "Hell." He pulled her on tiptoe and slanted his mouth over hers.

Need washed over her, a wild force she had no control of. She moaned in return and threw her arms around his neck, parting her lips for him.

He swept his tongue inside, dancing it back and forth over hers. She wiggled closer, fitting her hips to his and finding him once again bulging with arousal. Her panties grew wet and her clothing too confining. She needed them to fall off immediately so she could be naked and underneath this man.

Or against a wall.

There was also the table...

He slid his hands down her spine and around her waist as he fed her kiss after kiss. Her mind slowed, drinking in each moment because it was her last. She couldn't let him kiss her again—they had a working relationship, and she knew how that would end.

Except Sean's kisses felt nothing like Bo's. Her ex's had been less passionate, even on their wedding night. And Sean smelled so good...

She locked her arms around his neck, and he lifted her, hitching her thighs high on his hips, never releasing her mouth. He thrust his tongue into her mouth in a mimicry of the sex act, and she was going to combust if she didn't get these clothes off—now.

Threading her fingers in his hair, she took his kisses, running her tongue along his lower lip and raising a masculine growl from him that sent goosebumps skittering all over her body.

"You're fucking incredible. Everything about you," he said between her nibbling bites.

When she reached the corner of his lips and she flicked her tongue there, his expression grew fierce and he slammed his mouth over hers hard.

"Sean..." It came out as a whimper or a coo, and Elise was not a cooing woman. She'd never cooed in her life. What was he doing to her?

The pressure must be getting to her. She didn't just fuck men, but they'd just had a huge breakthrough and were getting caught up in the excitement.

Swept away, more like.

Off the dining room was a flight of stairs, and he turned toward it, still cradling her in his arms. In fifteen steps they'd be at the top and either of their beds were so close.

Oh God, did she want to sleep with him?

Hell yes. Her body was on fire for it, her nipples throbbing, tightly puckered. Her pussy slick with need and every other inch of her body screaming out for Sean's touch.

"My room or yours?" he asked halfway up the stairs.

"Yours." She dipped her head to suck on his neck, salty-sweet.

He groaned and took the steps faster, skipping two and three at a time. At the top, he shot forward, propelled by lust. He supported her weight in one strong arm as he fiddled with something, and she realized it was the door. A second later, he kicked it in.

Kicked. It. In.

Ripples of desire had her pussy clenching as he slammed the door shut behind them and strode to the bed. She expected to feel the mattress beneath her but he stood there, holding her.

"Tell me you want this." His voice sounded as if he'd guzzled ground glass.

Dammit, now he was making her stop and think. She didn't want her analytical brain to kick in. She was more than happy to let go and just feel.

His dark eyes glistened with desire as he looked at her. Gold flecks seemed to sparkle brighter. "Make the choice, Elise."

She wasn't letting him walk away now. Her libido, now awakened, was an insatiable beast. She grinned. "You don't know what you're asking for."

That bad-boy grin flashed again, making her heart roll over. "Oh yes, I fucking do." He laid her on the bed and stood at the side, hands fisted. For a long second, she feared he'd walk away from her. But his heated gaze swept her from head to foot and then he reached for her sneakers.

"I know exactly what I'm getting with you, *cher*."

She bit into her lower lip as he removed her shoes and then made slipping off her socks insanely erotic. Her breaths came in heavy pants, and she makes us t she might come on the spot the moment he reached for her sweatpants.

Instead he reached between his shoulder blades and tugged off his shirt. Baring the muscles she'd admired—no, drooled over—during their run. And now she'd get to touch them, lick them...

"Come here." She beckoned with a finger.

His eyelids drooped. "Fuck, I want you."

"Then take me."

He didn't need a gold-lettered invitation. He lowered himself over her, taking control of her mouth as he closed his finger and thumb around her nipple. She arched, her cry lost to his kiss. Heat sparked inside her, running along her nerves like liquid fire. When he reached under her top and located her bare breast, she pinched her eyes shut hard and lost herself to sensation.

"So hard for me. Jesus," he ground out, moving his hand across her ribcage to her other breast.

She couldn't get enough of his kisses, his touch. She reached between them and found the button of his jeans. He locked his fingers around her wrist and moved it up and over her head, pinning her to the bed.

"Not yet. I need all the control I can get with you."

His admission shouldn't slam her so hard or burrow so deep. He was a playboy, all Knights were, and he probably used that line on every girl he took to bed. But her body lit up at his words, and there was no going slow on her part.

She dug the nails of her free hand into his shoulders and yanked him down on her. Feeling his weight only heightened her need. She spread her legs, drawing him against her center.

"Hell, I can feel your heat. Fuck."

She loved how he spoke in grunts and monosyllables. It made her feel desired, but later when she analyzed it, she'd know it was just words. But for now, she had a gorgeous hunk of a special ops man between her thighs and she wasn't going to think too much.

Especially when he was soooo good with his fingers.

When he pulled off her T-shirt, she watched his face. Men liked the way her body looked, and she was damn proud of it. She'd worked hard for it, after all.

His eyes hooded as he stared at her. Suddenly, a wolfish grin took over his face, and he stripped her entirely.

She reached for his jeans again, but he wasn't having any of that. He grabbed her hands and pinned them to her sides as he hovered over her. Holding her gaze, he parted his lips and sucked her nipple into his mouth.

Heat blazed through her, and she bucked off the mattress. With soft pulls of his mouth, he drove her from wild to wildfire in zero point two seconds. Juices squeezed from her folds, and if he didn't get inside her soon—

"Oh God, Sean!" He bit into her nipple, leaving her humming with a brand-new need. She curled her fists into the bed and rocked upward to get closer to the torment of his mouth.

His dark gaze lingered on hers as he drew his teeth over the tip of her breast before moving to the other one. When he drew it into his mouth, she cried out.

The bed shook, and she realized he was chuckling.

"You're laughing at a time like this?" She gasped as he swirled his tongue around her hard peak.

"I like an enthusiastic woman."

What he probably meant was the entire inn of nerdy code-crackers could hear her screaming with pleasure and she'd never be able to show her face again. But she didn't care. His mouth was the stuff of legend.

He teased and lapped at her nipple until she arched off the bed. To her disappointment, he didn't graze her with his teeth again, but the light kisses he spattered over her stomach made up for it.

He reached her mound, the trim fuzz as dark as the five o'clock shadow sprouting on his angular jaw. "You're soaking."

"I..."

"Let me taste you."

Without waiting for her acquiescence, he flattened his tongue over her slit. Heat curled through her clit and spiked deep inside. She threw her head back on another cry.

"Sean!"

"Mmm. I fucking knew you'd taste this sweet." He took his time, licking up one outer lip and barely skimming her clit to lick down the other. When he fixed her in his gaze and plunged his tongue into her pussy, she came off the bed.

No man had ever gone down on her the first time. The fact that Sean was enjoying it—

eyes shut and groaning as he explored her entire pussy from top to bottom—made her expectations of what was to come rocket skyward.

The man knew how to sex a girl up.

"Holy… shit." She gasped as he sucked on her clit and eased one long finger inside her. Her inner walls clenched around him, spilling more juices. He pulled his finger out and painted her with them.

And then licked her clean.

More profanities filled her mind, but she was too far gone to utter them. She gave herself up to his lips and tongue. When he eased two fingers—then three—into her channel, she quaked on the edge of ecstasy.

He seemed to delight in keeping her there, on the brink of coming but not allowing it to happen.

Arrogant man.

She thumped a heel on his spine, and the bed shook with his rumble of laughter again. He pressed his three fingers up against her inner wall, and juices flooded his hand.

"How… are you… making me do that?"

"I have a few tricks up my sleeve." He massaged that erogenous zone until so much pressure grew in her core that there was no way to remain still. She bucked, ground her hips and finally begged.

"Let me come. Please, Sean."

He lowered his tongue to her clit again, licking her slow even as he finger-fucked her fast. Elise hovered in a headspace of bliss for ten seconds, twelve…and then a wave of orgasm hit her so hard that she had no air to scream.

* * * * *

Sean's fingers were soaked and his mouth wet with Elise's sweet juices, but he wasn't finished with her. He'd never wanted to give a woman so many orgasms, and he wasn't stopping until she came again.

Only then might he consider removing his jeans and gliding into her. Knowing once he felt her tight heat, he'd have all of five strokes before he exploded, he had to restrain himself.

She bucked into his mouth, and he found a new rhythm, tonguing her slow and then fast. Her pussy pulsated around his fingers and under his lips, and damn if his cock wasn't leaking pre-cum in a constant stream.

She twisted the covers in her fist, her stomach muscles leaping as he pushed her higher and higher.

He couldn't tear his gaze from her beautiful face. Contorted in pleasure, her cheeks a darker hue with her flush. Her lips were swollen from his kisses or her biting them or both.

He moaned against her pussy, and she pushed off the bed again, sculpted inner thighs quivering. Pressing his fingertips up into that magic spot had her spilling more juices for him. By the time he was finished, he wanted her hoarse from her cries and in need of hydration.

His chest tightened, and he doubled his efforts. A new emotion had his mind reeling, but he didn't have time to stop and examine what it could be. He toyed her clit back and forth with his tongue and slowly removed his fingers from her pussy.

"Ahhhh."

He plunged them deep again.

"AHHHH."

Suddenly, he didn't give a damn about the intercepted messages or the mission. OFFSUS had it set up that they received each new bit of intel automatically and Hawk no longer needed to carry anything. Sean's sole goal in the world was to make Elise come apart for him until she collapsed.

94

The only worthwhile achievement of his lifetime, as far as he was concerned.

He grinned as she tugged at his hair, pushing his head down where she wanted it. "Happy to oblige," he drawled.

"Sean!" She shook, on the verge of release, and he took mercy. Opening his mouth wide over her pussy and fingering her with rhythmic strokes. He was already tuned into her body's needs, and while that wasn't anything new with him and his lovers, he felt like he'd broken some barrier in Elise.

She sucked in sharply and held her breath. Arching underneath him and then jerking her hips fast as her pussy squeezed around his fingers. He didn't slow his torment until she dropped to the mattress.

Licking her slick folds, he watched the peace and ecstasy spread over her beautiful features.

"Good?" he rumbled from his perch between her thighs.

She nodded and opened her eyes to pierce him in her glazed stare. "Acceptable."

He reared up. "Acceptable? You're still shaking and haven't stopped for half an hour."

Her smile was pure teasing woman, a side of her he hadn't seen before. And damn, did he like it. From the start, he'd known she was a passionate female, but he suspected there was much more in Elise he hadn't tapped.

Yet.

He did an erotic pushup and moved to stare down into her eyes. "I guess I'll just have to keep working to please you." With lips still damp from her juices, he kissed her. She melted, opening her mouth for him to sweep his tongue inside. Passion ignited, and he couldn't kick his jeans off fast enough.

She lay watching, dark hair mussed around her oval face and lower lip trapped in her teeth. He'd had a lot of women's eyes on him before, but somehow having Elise appreciating the hard work he'd put into his body meant more.

As her gaze roved over his chest and shoulders, down to his abs, he reached into his jeans and drew out his hard length. Fuck, he could barely touch his throbbing flesh. A few strokes of his fist and it'd be all over.

Her eyes widened and she pushed onto her elbows. "No way can that be all you."

"Who else could it belong to, *cher*?" He grinned and shoved his jeans and underwear off in one hurried move, giving her a full frontal view.

She wet her lips, tongue darting out to run along them. His cock jerked, and he gripped it at the base, giving it one smooth stroke of his fist.

"Hell," he heard her mutter under her breath.

He made a show of turning to the side and bending for his wallet and the stash of condoms there. Early in his military career, he'd learned to never leave home without more than one. Because if he got a chance to fuck, he was fucking all night long.

From the corner of his eye, he saw Elise watching his every move. He made a show of tearing open the packet with his teeth.

"Were you a stripper before you were a Marine?"

He flashed a grin and rolled the condom over his cock in one jerk of his hand. Then he walked toward the bed, his shaft jutting toward her. The constrictive rubber made him wish he could tear it off and sink into her bareback.

When he reached the side of the bed, she pushed to her knees and slipped her arms around his neck. Kissing him with an urgency that fed into his desires until his precious control was threatened. He had to take action before it was too late.

He lifted her and stretched out on the bed, settling her over his cock. As the tip of his erection poised at the quick of her, she gave a harsh breath.

"God, Sean. Why do I want this so bad?"

Her admission stole his mind. With a growl, he jerked his hips upward as she sank over his cock. Each inch filling her, stretching her. They shared a loud moan, and she took him completely, the soft globes of her ass skimming his groin.

He cupped her backside in his hands and urged her to move. As she eased upward, he locked his gaze to her face, drinking in the pleasure he saw rippling across her features. His balls clenched, and he tightened his grip on her toned ass.

"Ohh," she breathed out as she sank down on him again. The motion caused her breasts to jiggle, and he cupped one, strumming his thumb back and forth over the distended tip as she began to set a pace.

Rolling her hips, head tossed back, her body the sexiest he'd ever laid eyes on. Everything about her set him off, stripped away his control.

She rocked her hips, and the tip of his cock bottomed out. They both groaned, loudly.

A giggle sounded in the hallway, and Elise's gaze locked on his. "We're noisy."

"I was thinking you're not noisy enough." He twitched his hips, digging his cock deep. She answered with a louder moan.

"This is… unprofessional."

"I'm not a professional. But thank you for the compliment." His joke came out with a hitch of his breath.

She shuddered as she withdrew on his length again. He watched his cock slide out of her sweet, wet pussy. Her pussy he could still taste on his lips and tongue. Her tight, hot, clenching pussy…

"Fuck, *cher*. I'm too close. Hold still."

Those words seemed to be the challenge she needed to double her efforts. She braced her hands on his shoulders, her weight feeling like nothing atop him, and she moved faster. Taking him deeper with each passing stroke until her movements grew jerky.

He grabbed her hips and fucked up into her fast and hard, watching her face for the point of no return. When he saw her eyes widen and her mouth fall open on an O of surprise, he let go.

Roaring out his release as it shot up from the base of his spine, his mind blanked to anything but Elise's tight body and the squeeze of her inner walls around him, drawing out spurt after spurt.

* * * * *

Elise watched Sean's backside disappear into the bathroom, the sight of his strong form resonating within her for what... the fifth time? How could she go from completely satisfied to wanting him again after one glance at his muscled body? Or his sparkling eyes *or* that crooked smile?

She pulled the sheet over her nudity and thought about what she was doing. It was still daylight, and she was thinking about spending the day—and night—in bed with her hot sidekick.

Bo would kill her when he found out.

No, she could never share this type of information. Sure, she knew a bit about the women he dated but not details. And something about the way Bo and Sean faced off told her to keep the news to herself.

She heard the water running and a second later, the bathroom door opened. Sean appeared, looking mussed and sexy as hell. A sprinkling of dark hair on his chest drawing her gaze down to the thin trail running straight to—

He made a gruff noise that snapped her attention to his face.

"I'm glad you like what you see." Great— his arrogant swagger as he crossed the room to the bed was all she needed. Now he'd thump his chest and brag about his conquest.

She drew her knees to her chest, keeping the sheet over her bare parts. "I could say the same for you."

He dived into bed, jostling her so the sheet fell away. He dragged it down and rolled against her, pulling her flush to his body and then flipping the sheet over them both. She blinked at how fast he'd managed that maneuver. Was that a special ops thing or a gigolo thing?

Plastered against his big body, she stiffened. He ignored her posture and began to rub small circles from her shoulders to lower back. By the time he started up again, she relaxed.

Okay, this wasn't just a victory fuck. This was couples stuff, and she didn't do couples.

He seemed to sense her thoughts, drawing her closer and pressing a kiss to her temple. "You're an amazing woman, you know that?"

Oh no—not the compliments. She had to get out of this bed.

"Um, thanks?"

"I don't just mean that hip action, baby. Though *Dieu* knows, that had me on the edge of my control."

A quizzical smile hit her lips, and she lifted a hand to toy with his chest hair. Maybe she was overthinking things—she'd jumped into bed with him spontaneously. Who said she had to complicate things now and make it more than the fun she'd set out to claim for herself?

Besides, she was a grown woman. She knew her course in life, and men weren't part of the equation. Maybe someday, she'd settle down with someone and have a family, but for now, she was happy with her independence.

"Your mind makes a noise when you're thinking, you know that?" His rumbled words jarred her. She stopped tracing his sculpted pec and looked at him.

Amusement crinkled the corners of his eyes. Man, why did men get to have all the good things in life? They got better with age while women spent hundreds on creams to keep the same smile lines from taking over their faces.

"Now you're glaring at me," he said.

She smacked him across the shoulder. "I was thinking."

"You're deciphering us."

Her brows drew together. "There is no us."

"Oh, but there is an us. Many orgasms between the two of us."

She smacked him again, causing him to shake with laughter. "We've finished what we set out to do and got carried away."

"Is that what you call all the chemistry you've been battling for days?"

She rolled onto her back and stared at the simple white ceiling. Light played across it, making her think of dinner on the patio or their run on the shore. She had to admit they got along in many ways, and their romp in bed had been an extension of that same chemistry.

"We work together," she stated.

"Uh huh. And play together."

"Sean, I'll just come out and say it—this is a one-time deal. One day—"

"And one night," he cut her off.

"That's to be determined. But we won't see each other after this."

"We'll see." When he smiled, her heart pattered faster. How did he cause such a reaction in her body? It must be because she'd been alone too long. She was just acting on her needs, taking what she wanted.

With the hottest man she'd ever met.

"What I was trying to say before you thought it important to let me know you'll never be in my bed again, is that you're amazing, Elise. The smartest woman I've ever known, and that's saying something since I have some pretty clever sisters."

She'd been told this before but coming from him, it touched her. She lowered her eyes to stare at the angles of his jaw. Dark stubble shadowed it, giving him a more dangerous look. But she didn't need to guess at how lethal this man was. He'd killed to protect, yet he'd touched her with indescribable tenderness.

He ran his hand down her spine to cup her buttocks. The roughness and heat of his hand sent spears of lust straight to her pussy. He kneaded her behind, his mouth at her ear.

"I'm an ass man, and this one..." he squeezed, "is everything." His dirty words coupled with his touch rendered her stupid, and she didn't even realize he'd rolled her onto her stomach until the sheet tickled her cheek.

He sat up, she assumed to stare at her bottom. When he began to trail his fingers over her globes, she sighed with pleasure. The light, ticklish touch acted like a stress reducer, and she flung her arms overhead. He moved his fingers to the top of the muscle, gently massaging, before gliding along the outer curve. As he reached the undercurve, her nipples hardened and her pussy contracted.

But when he dipped his fingers between her thighs, brushing her wetness, she let out a moan.

"Still so wet for me, *cher*. I can't tell you how much that pleases me."

Did she want to please him? God yes. And as soon as she could get her mind back, she wanted to flatten him to the bed and taste that big, hard cock of his too. If she was getting one experience with Sean, she was going all in.

He drew his fingers out of her pussy and ran them over her buttocks. Her body relaxed, and her thighs fell apart. So when he dragged his fingertips down her ass crack, she was suddenly so… exposed.

His caress against her anus drew a shocked gasp from her, and she tightened her muscles.

Warm breath washed over her neck. "Relax, baby. Let me learn what you like."

"I… don't like that."

"You know this?"

She didn't. And she could still feel his touch — there. It aroused her.

"Your body is so fine." He continued exploring, loosening her muscles and knocking down her walls again. Surely he wouldn't touch her there now. She issued a soft sigh and closed her eyes, reveling in the relaxation of her muscles after long hours seated in front of a screen.

Her breaths came slower. His touch slowed too. So when he ran his finger over her netherhole a second time, she gasped.

He placed his lips at her ear. "Tell me you don't like the way this feels, Elise." He paused with his fingertip on her anus. The barest of pressure.

And damn if she didn't want more.

Her nipples hardened against the mattress, and her pussy clenched. He didn't move his finger away, only rested it over her most intimate spot for a long minute.

Then he moved on. Tracing down to her undercurve again and back around. To her opposite buttocks. Leaving her stomach quaking with anticipation of when he'd stroke that spot again.

Oh God, what had he turned her into?

She wasn't a prude by any means, but this wasn't even something Bo had done with her.

Her belly quivered when he reached her seam once more. His hot finger blazed a path down between her cheeks. When he reached her pucker, she pushed back.

He groaned, a gritty sound that raised the hairs on her nape. The erotic noise buried deep in her even as he pressed harder on that place. What would it feel like if he slid his finger inside her?

She let her thighs part naturally, giving him more access.

"Feels good, doesn't it, *cher*?"

A moan escaped her, and she couldn't bring herself to care.

He teased her by continuing his massage, even working down the backs of her thighs. By the time he reached the spot she most wanted touched, she was out of her head.

"Sean..." she whispered, "touch me. Please."

He released a rough noise that only turned her on more, before circling his finger around her pucker. Need splashed across her senses, and a deep ache took hold. Some unseen end hung within reach and yet so far away.

Each light, skittering brush of his finger thrust her higher toward a pleasure unlike anything she'd known before. "I wish I had some lube," he said quietly.

"Oh God, Sean. Forget the lube! Just slide your finger in me."

A beat of silence followed, and then, "Fucking hell." He knelt behind her, drawing her hips high in the air. She gripped the sheets, prepared for whatever he did to her. Even if he gave her that big cock of his... she just needed... more.

"Christ, you're beautiful. Open to me. So primed." His rough words hit her belly and her heart somersaulted. But she didn't have time to think on those things because he eased his finger inside her. Past the tight ring.

She buried her face in the sheets. It was so good, so unexpected.

He slipped a bit farther in, and she understood why he mentioned the lube. It would make it soooo good. But he was gentle, and she was too horny to care if this wasn't the ideal situation.

He worked his finger to the first knuckle. Then to her surprise, he slipped in the rest of the way.

"Oh God," she cried.

"Oh fuck," he answered.

Then he reached between her thighs with his other hand and began massaging her clit while extracting his finger with mind-bending slowness. She was going to die of pleasure. But at least she'd die happy.

* * * * *

She was an ass virgin—he was sure of it. From the tight clench of her body to her uninhibited responses, he knew it. And the fact that she was letting him explore her this way raised some primal need to claim.

He watched her body for cues as he slowly finger-fucked her ass and rubbed her clit. The moans leaving her left no question as to how he was making her feel. His cock bobbed against his abs, stiffer than it had ever been. If he listened to his body, he'd be buried in that tight heat right now. But she wasn't ready, and he wouldn't hurt her.

With each move of his fingers, she quaked a little more until the whole bed shook with it.

"Sean… it's… I'm…"

"Let it come, *cher*."

"It's going to be… big."

"I know. Let it happen." He thrust his finger in once more and she stiffened, not breathing. One hard pulsation hit his finger and then she was screaming, contracting around him with an orgasm so big that her screams could be heard way out at Colonel Jackson's place.

As soon as the final tremor left her, he drew his fingers free and reached over the side of the bed for a condom. He had to get inside her—now.

She lay still, face down, but when he dragged her ass back into the air, she glanced over her shoulder. Perspiration dampened her hair and her eyes were wild with need. "Take me, Sean. I need you to fuck me."

"You got it." He barely ground out the words before he was balls-deep, churning his hips toward an end so huge that it would erase all the other women who'd come before her.

She reached back to grasp his hip, guiding him in with more forceful thrusts. A roar rose up in his throat and he tipped over the edge. The first spurt would have hit her neck if he weren't wearing a condom, but she was bucking, taking everything he had to give. Sapping him.

And damn if he wasn't going to give his all. He was aware of her orgasm stuttering to a stop as his last jet of come left him.

They collapsed and he rolled off so he didn't crush her.

"I can't move," she murmured.

"After that, no wonder." He curled around her body, her back fitting so perfectly to his front. His eyes drifted shut, and he was aware of their breathing. How it synced.

How unusual that was.

Long seconds passed and then he kissed her nape. "I'm going to clean up. Don't move."

"I couldn't if I wanted to." Her words were slurred with exhaustion, and his chest might have swelled a bit, knowing what he'd done to her.

When he got up, he was shocked to see how dark the room had become. Hours must have passed, and he'd lost all track of time. The messages they'd decoded would be in the right hands by now, and his brothers would be dispatched soon. Sean's work with Elise was finished, and he had no excuse to not join his team.

But until he got that phone call, he was staying right here in this room with Elise.

He washed up and crawled back into bed. As soon as he stretched out, she turned to him and gave him a wicked smile, eyes snapping.

"What do you know that I don't?" he asked with a smile of his own.

"This." She slid down his body and gripped his cock at the base, swallowing him to the root.

Chapter Five

Sean made a waving motion, and Dylan and Chaz jumped up from the weeds and took off toward the warehouse. Sean kept his finger on the trigger of his weapon, ready to take out any threat to his team, and secretly hoping he could shoot the asshole responsible for dragging him out of Elise's bed.

She'd been so soft, warm… fragrant. He could still smell her on him, though he'd long ago sweat off her scent. He'd walked out on her without a fucking word, and while Ben might be known for the love-'em-and-leave-'em life before he found Dahlia, Sean was not.

More than likely he'd thoroughly severed any chances of getting back in Elise's good graces. She was smart and hardheaded. He couldn't imagine a woman like that not holding grudges.

He prayed that the memory of him cuddling her between wild sex sessions was enough to keep her from hating him.

"Holy shit, Thunder. You were right." Chaz's words filtered through his comms unit and into his ear. "This place is like the warhead warehouse."

In a crouching position, Sean jerked and had to grip the abandoned vehicle he was hiding behind to remain upright. When he'd taken Dylan and Chaz and split off from Ben, Rocko and Roades and headed to the farm, he'd followed his gut instincts. Apparently, he needed to do that more often, because he'd led his team directly to the warheads they'd been searching for.

"All three of 'em?" he asked his brothers.

Chaz's voice came back, quiet and clear. "Two. Third's still in the wind."

"I'm coming in," Sean said.

"Negative," Dylan said at once. "Keep the lookout. Chaz is checking to see if they're armed."

Sean's heart slammed his ribs. Darkness closed in around them, and the air was scented with the fresh rain that had just fallen and growing things crushed under his boots.

A minute later, another voice filled his ear. Since this comms had a range of a mile, that must mean Ben and the others headed this direction.

"What's the word?" Ben asked.

"We got them," Sean reported.

A beat of silence. "All three?"

"Two."

"And they're disarmed," Dylan added with a note of victory in his tone.

A low cheer flooded Sean's hearing, coming from Rocko and Roades. But they weren't out of danger yet—whoever owned this place would obviously have a problem with the stolen missiles being discovered.

Sean started to remind them of this when Ben said, "Great—here comes the Knight Ops Pee-Wee Team."

Sean peered into the darkness but couldn't detect any movement. "Who?"

"Fuckin' Jackson saddled us with backup. We met up with them an hour or so ago, told them we can handle it. But they're clinging to us like flies."

"Who the hell's heading the Pee-Wees?" Sean scanned the property again just as his brothers exited the steel building, cloaked by camo and darkness as they navigated the yard to where Sean hunkered down by the dilapidated Chevy.

Dylan's teeth flashed white in his face, darkened with grease paint. "Never saw a warhead in person."

"Let's hope we see at least one more, and soon," Chaz said, crowding close to Sean and looking to him. "Who the hell are these Pee-Wees?"

114

"They're the assholes who'll be doing the paperwork since we did all the work finding the warheads." Sean's dry tone had them all chuckling, even Ben.

"To answer your question, Thunder, Hawk's heading the Pee-Wees."

Sean sobered. "That asshole?" Hawk wasn't exactly a small man either, so Sean's amusement shot up a notch thinking of him on a team the Knight Ops were calling the Pee-Wees.

"For the record, we can hear you motherfuckers," Hawk's voice came in over theirs.

Sean did a mental eye roll. The last thing they needed was that guy's cocky attitude on the scene. He checked their surroundings again before directing Ben and the guys to come in.

As they scattered to search for the third warhead, Sean held his position. From what he could tell, the farmhouse was abandoned. There wasn't a cluck of a chicken or a soft knicker of a horse to break the night, and Sean didn't think it was because the animals were so well-behaved. There simply weren't any.

But that didn't mean someone wasn't sleeping inside the house and just hadn't yet realized they were there. When he did, he was sure to bring friends.

Dylan nudged him. "You get a piece of that code cracker?"

Sean swung his gaze to him, an odd shiver in his gut at the mention of Elise. "Who says I was interested?"

Dylan snorted. "Why else did you push me aside and take over? It wasn't to learn a new skill."

"Fuck you."

Another low chuckle sounded from Dylan, but he abruptly cut it off as four men emerged from the shadows to join them. This time Sean did roll his eyes—Hawk had his chest puffed up like a fucking rooster.

"We only need you to get out your pens and get ready to do the paperwork, boys." Sean's statement made Hawk's head snap around. The man's dark eyes glittered. What Elise had seen in the guy was beyond Sean. But he didn't like thinking of Hawk kissing her, touching her.

"Watch yourself, Thunder," Hawk said, low.

Ignoring his position, Sean stood, placing his chest inches from Hawk's. They glared at each other.

"I think it's you who'd better watch yourself." Sean wanted to tell him to stay away from Elise, but she'd told him that they were

116

close friends, and Hawk would go running back with Sean's words.

He opened his mouth to say more, but a deadly *thump* ripped through the night. The bullet peeled up the turf inches to the right of where he and Hawk stood. Sean hit the dirt, scope fixed in the direction from where the shot had come.

"Shot fired. Chaz, Dylan, circle around and come in on this fucker's left. See if you can get eyes on him." Sean's orders drew a grunt from Hawk, who was lying beside him, in a sniper position using his leg to stabilize him to make the shot.

If he got one first—Sean prided himself on being quick on the trigger.

Spotting the faintest outline of a man's leg, Sean estimated how far up his heart would be and took the shot.

At the same time, Hawk bumped his elbow as he squeezed off his own shot.

A scream of pain told Sean he'd hit his mark, but anger boiled in his temples as he whirled on the man who'd purposely bumped him so he could look like the fucking hero.

"You asshole, I should fucking shoot off your kneecaps for that." Sean dropped his weapon and reached for Hawk's throat.

Hawk tossed his rifle down too and swung his fist at Sean's nose.

He dodged and closed his fingers around Hawk's thick neck. It would take a while to strangle him to death, but Sean had big hands and there was plenty of land to bury the cocky ass on.

Dylan stepped between them, delivering an elbow to Sean's midsection and knocking the breath from him even as he raised his rifle butt over Hawk's brow. "Don't make me knock your ass out, Hawk. Now I don't know what happened just now, but we've got a man bleeding or worse on the ground and possibly more threats."

Sean pushed out a low growl and stepped back from Hawk, bending to retrieve his weapon. When Hawk attempted the same, Sean set his boot down on Hawk's fingers.

"Both of ya are dumbasses," Dylan murmured and moved into stealth mode, running up on the man on the ground.

Sean stared down at Hawk. "Don't fuck with me."

Hawk grunted but said nothing. Sean lifted his foot and they sprang forward at the same time, securing the area.

As Ben pounced on the man who'd been shot, howls of pain were interspersed with

Ben's sharp commands. Sean focused on everything going on, but the back of his mind still burned with fury over Hawkeye's actions. When he got the man alone—

"Thunder, make the call to Jackson. Tell him this idiot claims to have purchased two warheads for his collection. Ninja, Rocko, take the Pee-Wees and search the place."

Sean pushed out a laugh at the mention of the Pee-Wees, and Hawk glared at him. Sean arched a brow and waited for him to walk away from him. When he did, Sean resisted the urge to swing his rifle butt at the back of the man's thick skull.

Yeah, Elise must have been blind to have married that thing. And Sean didn't even want to dwell on the fact that they were still friends.

* * * * *

Dinner. Pick u up at 7.

Elise read the text from Bo and sighed at his high-handedness. He still thought he could control her life, and up until a few days ago, she wouldn't have minded a dinner date.

So what had changed?

She leaned back in her deck chair situated on the miniscule balcony of her apartment. It overlooked a grassy lawn and part of the dirty alley behind the building, but she rested against the back to stare at the sky. A thin wisp of a cloud floated by, for some reason reminding her of a ship.

Which oddly led her to thoughts of Sean, probably because he'd sailed out of her life as quickly as he'd crash-landed into it. After a very long, sweaty night of passionate sex, she'd woken to find him gone.

She crossed her legs and closed her eyes, but memories of that night bombarded her. Sighs of pleasure, cries of ecstasy. The salty-sweet taste of his body. Then that four-a.m. shower that would live on in her mind forever...

But he'd walked out of her life and she hadn't even received a text from him, and he couldn't claim he didn't know her number. He'd charmed her with his crinkle-eyed smiles and his playfulness—then after he got what he wanted from her, he'd run out.

She had a feeling if she rustled up a few of his lovers, they'd tell her similar stories. Elise wasn't different and definitely not special.

She cracked an eye open, but the wisp of cloud was gone. Just like Sean.

These odd moments of down-time always unnerved her and left her too much time to contemplate her life. OFFSUS didn't have work for her every day, but when they called, she had to drop everything and run to help. That meant she couldn't hold down a part-time job just to cure the boredom of days sitting here on her lousy balcony.

Dwelling on Sean definitely wasn't something she had time for—he'd only been a fuck. Someone to scratch an itch, and a damn beautiful man too. Who wouldn't have taken a chance on him?

If she'd met him at a bar, a one-night stand wouldn't have warranted a passing thought about the man. But since they'd worked together—hell, shared meals, jokes and too many long, heated looks to count—she felt betrayed.

Ugh, not that word. She was too soft for her own good, and even years as a Marine hadn't knocked the sweet Louisiana girl out of her. She still harbored dreams of finding Mr. Right and sharing a life.

Not that she'd ever let her mind go there with Sean Knight. No, he was never Mr. Right in her eyes. In fact, he was Mr. All Wrong from the very start. Yet she'd let him into more than her bed.

Dammit, she had to cut off these thoughts of him and get on with her life. Sunbathing on her tiny balcony wasn't helping her any. She had to get up, find something to do.

Maybe go for a run.

That brought her mind right back to Sean and his gorgeous muscles rolling under his tanned skin as he sprinted across the shore.

Great—now her nipples were hard too. She might as well try texting him and throwing herself at the guy. Her body's reactions were just as worthless to her.

She grabbed her phone and did the only thing she could think would help her close the book on those few days of her life once and for all. She texted Bo.

Can u meet now?

What's wrong? He responded immediately, as always. He never ignored her, made her feel important. Too bad they hadn't worked out because they seemed to perfect for each other. So what was it about Bo that *hadn't* been right?

Nothing's wrong. Just too much time on my hands.

I'll be there in 5.

As she went back inside and closed and locked the door leading to the balcony, she couldn't help but feel a little pitiful. If she were honest, she'd summoned Bo like other women would text a girlfriend asking them to bring a pint of Ben and Jerry's and join them for a break-up pity party.

Except it wasn't a breakup, she told herself for the umpteenth time. She and Sean were never a thing.

While she waited for Bo, she busied herself by tidying up the apartment, cleaning off the countertop and washing her breakfast plates. When she was placing the wet dishes on the draining rack, the door opened.

She turned to watch her ex striding toward her, eyes narrowed and a fierce expression on his rugged features.

"What happened?" he demanded, coming to a stop in front of her.

She craned her neck to meet his gaze. "Nothing happened. Just bored is all. I guess I need more jobs." She gave a faint giggle with no heart behind it.

He took her by the shoulders, forcing her to hold his stare. "You slept with that asshole."

She nearly swallowed her tongue. Once she could force air past her vocal cords, she said, "What? Why would you ask me that?"

"Because I saw how he looked at you. Fucking hell, I knew I shouldn't have left you alone with him!"

"Bo, calm down. I never said I slept with Sean." Her voice gave a suspicious wobble on his name.

"Jesus, and you've fallen for him." He released her shoulders and ran his fingers over his shaved head.

She gaped at him. Was he some kind of mind-reader? Because the link between friends, or exes, was far from telepathic. And there was no other way for Bo to know she'd slept with Sean—soooo many mind-blowing times—because she didn't even sport a red mark of beard burn from the man to give her away.

She shook her head. "I haven't fallen for anybody."

"But you did sleep with him." Bo's words came out flat.

For a pulsing second, she considered denying it. But he'd see right through her lie.

She nodded. "Yeah, I did."

He shoved out a breath and leaned against the countertop, staring at her without pause. She couldn't read the lights moving behind his eyes, but strangely she could have recited everything she'd seen in Sean's since the moment he'd sat beside her and started working with her.

Hell, maybe she *had* fallen for him.

No, she was just a wee bit obsessed. It was a crush, nothing more.

Except if he walked through the door right now, she'd shove Bo out and throw herself at the man.

Fuck, she was a little more than obsessed.

"I'm not even going to ask what you see in Knight."

The statement caught her off-guard. She wanted to ask Bo to tell her so she could understand herself. "You're not?"

"He's a low-life woman-schmoozing asshole with too much game. He knew exactly how to play you." Bo's eyes darkened, and Elise finally knew what her ex was thinking. She'd seen that look a few times, and it was always associated with her trying to stop him from breaking the neck of somebody who looked at her too long or even took liberties with her on a dance floor.

She put a hand on Bo's forearm, only to find the muscles and tendons leaping there. She looked down to find his fingers fisted.

"Bo," she said with warning in her tone, "don't. Sean didn't do anything wrong."

"Now you're defending the motherfucker to me?"

She raised a shoulder and let it drop before spinning away to look out of the glass door leading to the balcony.

For a long minute, silence reigned, and she wondered if she'd gone too far with the friendship thing with Bo. Maybe they weren't really able to forget they were once committed to each other, and he was affected by the knowledge she'd slept with Sean.

Though she could list half a dozen women Bo had been with.

She didn't *know* those women, however, and Bo did.

She spun, her words flying from her lips. "Look, I shouldn't have said anything."

"Go on this run with me."

She blinked. "What?"

"After I texted you about dinner, something fell into my lap, and I have to take care of it. I could use a sidekick."

Eyeing him, she said, "Sidekick?"

His face relaxed for the first time since walking through the door. "Backup. C'mon, Elise."

She jumped at the chance to get out of her apartment and her own head. "What is it? Am I dressed appropriately?"

"I'll arm you once we get there. You're perfect." He leaned in and kissed her between the brows, giving her warm fuzzy thoughts of Sean doing the same thing when he believed her asleep.

"All right, I'm in. Let me get my boots on."

"The ball-breakers with the steel toes, *cher.*"

More shades of Sean, his deep, low voice caressing her as he called her by the same endearment.

To cover her response, she arched a brow at Bo. "Whose balls am I breaking? I'd rather just shoot someone."

"If we're lucky, you'll get to do both. Hurry now. No time to waste."

* * * * *

Sean fiddled with the engine of the airboat, but it wasn't that healthy, stuttering and stalling out before he tweaked the carburetor again. Leave it to fucking Jackson to try to punish him for Hawk's bad behavior the other night. The guy was going to pay when Sean saw him next time too, for even telling the Colonel that Sean's shot had gone haywire.

The hot sun beat down on his shoulders as he messed with the engine until it purred like a happy gator gaping in the sun. Sean was actually looking forward to finding this fugitive just to take out his frustrations. And he *would* find him—nobody knew these swamps like he and his brothers. Dylan was already out there waiting for Sean to catch up. The rest of

Knight Ops, as far as he knew, were back at the cabin cracking open some cold ones and watching the game. Sean didn't mind taking this punishment, however. He needed the time to think, and his brothers hadn't stopped ribbing him about the incident.

But as far as he was concerned, he'd rather be out here tracking down an old-timer believed to have some knowledge of the third missile than deal with his sister, Lexi's latest boyfriend scandal. Wait till his brothers learned about it.

"Jesus Christ." The words, faint and several feet away, made Sean jerk to his feet, hand on his weapon.

"Don't even reach for it, dickhead." Hawk's voice made Sean's finger twitch. Better than burying the guy on a farm was weighting him and dropping him into the swamp. The gators would have his bones picked clean in a day, and nobody would ever be the wiser.

He opened his mouth to respond, but the breath punched from him when Hawk moved aside enough for him to see the small, tough, dark-haired beauty behind him.

Elise.

His lungs burned, screaming for air, but he couldn't find any, not when their gazes had locked.

She was dressed in jeans and a black T-shirt with heavy military-issue boots, and her hair was pulled back in a ponytail. Her eyes… God, she was gorgeous. And Sean's dick was twitching at the very sight of her.

He braced his feet wide as the pair approached.

"What the fuck're you doin' here?" Hawk asked, earning a sideways look from Elise.

A smile tugged at the corner of Sean's lips. Maybe the jerk would dig his own grave with Elise with his smart comments and she'd see him for what he was.

"Jackson ordered me to come." Sean stopped and stared at Hawk, not bothering to mention Dylan. "That son of a bitch. He sent you too?"

"Just me, not Elise. I asked her to come along as backup."

Sean stepped toward her, the urge to shield her strong. "You couldn't have found someone else?

"I wanted to come." When Elise spoke up, her soft voice burrowed deep into Sean. It hit his chest, dropping his heart and then slid downward to settle in his groin. His cock twitched again.

Sean couldn't read her expression—she'd wiped away the soft looks of pleasure they'd

shared the other night and replaced it with…
well, nothing. Her face was blank.

But then she glanced at Hawk, and a growl rose in Sean's throat. He barely bit it back. He could stand here with Hawk and prove who was the better man for the job—and for Elise.

A ripple in his ear brought his brother's voice into his head. "Did Hawk show up yet?"

"Excuse me for a minute. I have to check on something." Sean strolled back to the airboat and squatted before the engine, turning his face away from view so he could respond to Dylan.

"Yeah, why? Jackson sent him?"

Dylan laughed. "Nah. We figured he acted immaturely the other day when he hit your elbow as you took that shot."

"You know he claims it was an accident."

"Do you think it was an accident?"

Sean grunted.

"It was Rocko's idea that I get him here so you can show him you won't be bested. You're Knight Ops, man."

Sean worked over the opportunity in his mind, planning something simple and harmless that would hopefully get the guy off his back once and for all while still retaining his strict code of ethics and getting into the swamp with Dylan to find their guy.

130

"Thanks," Sean muttered and stood. As he headed back to meet Hawk and Elise, he jerked his jaw toward the path leading to the edge of the swamp and the half-ass airboat. "Can I talk to you for a minute?" he asked Hawk.

The man's eyes were flat black as he stared back. "Fine."

They left Elise, and he knew if he glanced back at her, he'd find her gaping at them. He walked some distance down the path so they were out of sight, but he wouldn't put it past her to follow. He had to act quick.

Reaching into his back pocket, he located the zip-ties he favored. Sizing up the man in front of him, he considered the best angle to take him down, bind him and then tie him to the nearest tree so he could take the airboat— and Elise.

Somehow, he needed to silence the fucker too, because any screaming would draw Elise's attention, and she probably wouldn't look kindly on Sean incapacitating her ex. Or friend. Whatever the hell she called Hawk.

Sean wished she wasn't associated with the jerkoff at all.

"Look, if you're going to harp on that wild shot you took the other night like an old woman, then—"

Sean leaped forward, got Hawk in a chokehold and slammed him to the ground before he could finish the sentence. Good thing—what he'd say was gonna piss Sean off anyway. Why was Hawk goading him? It was almost as if he was putting him through some kind of test.

In a flash, he had Hawk's hands bound behind his back and a sweaty bandana stuffed in his mouth. The man's eyes shot bullets as Sean zip-tied his ankles and feet, his soles of his boots together and a strap tightened across the toes so he couldn't wiggle out easily.

Then Sean dragged him a few feet to the nearest tree, around the bend and out of Elise's sight, and used rope to truss him to the trunk.

Perspiration poured down Sean's forehead, and he backhanded it away as he examined his efforts. Hawk glared, his face purple with fury.

"Elise and I will be back for you."

He made a noise but couldn't get any words past the dirty bandanna stuffed in his mouth.

Sean gave a nod and turned back down the path. To his relief, Elise stood in the same spot. Arms crossed, she looked angry—and adorable.

Knowing he had some explaining to do about his disappearance from her bed, Sean approached with caution. She *was* trained to kill, after all.

She glanced behind him. "Where's Bo?"

Her use of the nickname had Sean's hackles up again. Trying for nonchalance, he said, "We talked it out and he agreed I should take this mission." He looked into her eyes long and deep. "Will you join me? I'd like to talk to you."

She didn't drop her folded arms, but he saw her relenting. Finally, she nodded.

"Good. Are you armed?"

She gave him the what-do-you-think-I-am look and he ducked to hide his grin. "Climb aboard then. I think I've got the engine running more smoothly." Though to be abandoned in the swamp alone with a woman like Elise was an appealing idea.

She moved into the craft, as comfortable in this situation as she was in a fancy car. Damn, there was a lot about this woman to admire. Her toughness for one—her vulnerability for another. He'd witnessed both now, and they were equally hot in his eyes. He couldn't help but wonder if Hawk felt the same.

He started the airboat again and they shot off into the swamp. His orders were to find the fugitive who might lead to locating that third warhead. But he was also thrilled to have Elise alone, giving him time to make amends.

And he'd shown Hawk never to underestimate a Knight Ops man.

* * * * *

After ten minutes of riding, Sean cut the engine. Letting them float in the silence of the bayou.

Elise struggled with herself. The man seated by her was raising a need in her that was stronger than anything she'd experienced before. Too well she recalled their stolen moments at the inn.

And how he hadn't even left her a note or a text.

She folded her arms and waited for him to speak first, not trusting her own voice. From the corner of her eye, she saw him staring at her.

"*Cher*—"

"Don't call me that."

He closed his mouth with a snap and then pushed out a sigh. "Elise. I'm sorry for the way I left things."

"You didn't leave things any way at all—you just left."

"I was called to duty." He looked like he wanted to expand on that, but she knew whatever there was to be said about the mission was confidential. She'd been a Marine and married to Bo long enough to understand. She felt a little silly. She should have assumed Sean had left for a mission but when he hadn't even said goodbye, she'd lumped him right into the commitment-phobe category.

She wasn't going to let Sean off the hook so easily. She met his gaze, challenging him with her eyes. "You could have woken me and told me that."

"I..." He jammed his fingers through his hair, leaving it in delicious little ruffles that made her close her fists on the urge to touch it. "You're right. I could have woken you and told you I was going. I wasn't thinking, and I guess I'm not used to being with a woman who'd understand."

She squeezed her middle tighter, resisting the urge to shove him overboard. "I'm not one of your one-night stands."

His eyes registered his shock. During, between and after their sex-athon, she'd made it a point to tell him over and over that they were just having one night of fun. Now she'd really shoved her foot in her mouth, and unfortunately, it was a heavy, steel-toed boot, too big to speak around.

She avoided his gaze, but she didn't need to look at Sean to feel him. Moving toward her, his body heat washing up her side and sending her nipples into tight puckers. Oh, they remembered him very, very well.

"I know you're not a one-night stand, Elise."

"Do we have a mission here or not?"

"Look, I screwed up, and I'm sorry. I had the best night of my life with you, *cher*, and you clearly want to kick my ass."

She bit into her lower lip, chomping off the smile that wanted to form there.

"We've got about thirty seconds before we catch up to my brother—"

"Your brother?" she exclaimed.

"Yeah, Dylan's with me. Let's use these seconds wisely."

He inched closer, bringing his manly scent. A ripple of want ran through her, and she hardened herself against him. But when he pinched her chin in his rough thumb and fingertip and forced her to meet his stare, a quiet noise broke from her.

"Give me another chance." His words— hot and slick—found their target.

Between her legs.

Dammit, now she was wet and needy with the only man who'd made her come that way in the middle of the swamp and she wanted to forget all about locating the old Cajun fugitive and relive every lurid touch Sean had given her.

Her breaths came unsteady, and he zeroed in on her mouth, drawing closer. Closer.

"Hey, motherfucker! Thought you could best me?"

They jerked apart, and she looked around at the sound of Bo's voice.

"Jeezussss," Sean drawled, shaking his head at the sight of her ex standing on what appeared to be the only solid land, half-drenched and muddy.

Her surprise was replaced with shock. "Bo didn't leave the mission to you. What did you do to him?" She narrowed her eyes at Sean.

Unfazed, he looked back at her. "Bo didn't have this mission at all—Dylan tricked him in to get back at him for something he did to me last time. And I didn't do anything to him. Does he look harmed to you?"

"Well, no. But…" He did look pissed.

"Don't make me swim over to the boat and wring your neck, Knight," Bo called. "Come get me."

Sean put his hand on the engine again to start it. But he didn't make a move.

Elise widened her eyes at him. "You can't just leave him there."

"Sure I can."

She raised her brows.

"Fine," he practically growled.

He started the engine and motored over to where Bo stood calf-deep in water. Spanish moss clung to his clothing. Elise stood and reached out a hand for Bo to take, ignoring another primal noise from Sean.

Whatever was going on between these men was plain old stupid. Whether it was about her or their positions within OFFSUS was anybody's guess. If it was about her, she wasn't some prize to be won, and besides, if Bo had wanted her, he would have kept her. But they'd both been in agreement that a relationship wasn't for them. With the way he was acting, she had to keep reminding herself of this.

As for Sean… her slip of the tongue about the one-night stand was simply that—a slip. She didn't want more with him than what they'd shared.

Even if it had blown her mind and still made her body tingle from the aftershocks of orgasms given days before.

Bo took a seat next to her, and Sean's gaze riveted on the small crack of space between her and Bo's legs.

"Isn't this a pleasant day for a ride?" Bo's sarcasm earned him a glare from Sean.

She did her best to ignore their caveman antics and nodded toward the waterway. "Let's wrap this up so I can get away from both of you."

That statement had both Bo and Sean tossing her worried looks, but she ignored them completely. Sean got the boat up to speed again, and they navigated deep into the swamp. An occasional abandoned shack popped up here and there, and soon Sean stopped at one.

When Sean stood, Bo did too.

She started to get up, but Bo waved her back down. "We'll just scope this out. You get ready in case someone tries to escape."

She nodded and settled again, hand on her weapon.

They got out of the airboat, leaving it rocking gently as they disappeared into the shack. Water lapped at the sides of the boat and the spindly supports holding the structure out of the water. It looked about to collapse any moment, and she started to worry that it was too rotten to support two big men inside, when Bo returned.

He hopped into the boat and gunned the engine.

Elise cried out and when he didn't stop, just continued to hit the waterway at top speed, she punched him in the shoulder. Which was a mistake, because it was like striking concrete.

"Ow! Dammit, stop! What did you do to Sean?"

"He'll find his way back. Or he won't," he muttered under his breath and the roar of the airboat engine, but she heard. Bo was a true swamp rat, and he could play dirty.

She punched him again, aiming for his jaw this time, but he dodged her blow. "He'll prove what he's made of. I can't let you be with a guy who isn't worthy, can I? Now I know about Dylan's role in this too."

She glared at him. "Don't you dare bring him into your childish — "

He cut her off. "I was going to find him and follow our orders. Be nice see the face of any other Knight than Sean."

Elise fumed. This was going too far, and she was trapped firmly in the middle of their antics. She had half a mind to march into Colonel Jackson's office and demand they both be shot. Hell, she'd even waste the ammo on them.

Bo's grin didn't fade even after they'd located Dylan and then the Cajun and found him too drunk to be any good to them. But they did walk away with a couple names that had fallen in slurs from his slack lips right before he passed out.

Elise glanced back at the swamp, but there was no sign of Sean. Part of her thought about taking the boat back and finding him. But Bo was right — she couldn't go rescuing him. She needed a man who was stronger than that.

I guess he'll show me if I'm worth fighting for.

She raised her fist to her lips, hiding her smile. Sean had asked for another chance. Whether or not she was willing to give that to him hovered on his return. She had no doubt a man like Sean could get out of any situation, but whether or not he wanted to deal with her dirty-player, guard-dog ex-husband was another story.

After a long drive back to her apartment, Bo cut the engine and looked at her warily. "Look, about Knight—"

She held up a hand, silencing him. "What I do with Sean Knight is none of your business."

He stared at her for a long moment. "Seriously, Elise? You're more to me than a friend. Hell, you're family. Always have been."

Touched and irritated at the same time, she shook him off. "If I want to sleep with the entire Knight Ops team, I can. You're not my keeper, and you can't just make love interests disappear, Bo."

His brows shot up. "Love interest? The entire Knight Ops team? Jesus, Elise. Tell me you're kidding."

She leveled a stare at him that had him backpedaling. "I know you're not going to have a Knights orgy. But dammit, Sean? That little prick—"

Her warning groan cut him off. "I'm going inside and change so I can go for a run and try to work out some of this anger, Bo."

"You still want to grab dinner?"

She pressed her lips together.

"Okay, I get it. I'll text you later?"

"Fine." She got out of the vehicle. If she was lucky, she'd showed both men in her life how they needed to operate around her and that changes needed to be made.

Chapter Six

"What… the… fuck?"

"Lexi Knight! Just because you have Marines for brothers doesn't mean you have to talk like one of them." Their *maman's* shrill cry came from the front of the house as Sean sneaked in the back door and past Lexi.

He held a finger to his lips and pointed toward the upstairs.

"What happened to you?" Lexi whispered.

"Got caught in the swamp. Walked most of the day to get back." He was filthy and smelly—and he wanted nothing more than to get even with Hawk. Right after he paid Elise a visit and showed her exactly what he wanted from her.

Which was everything.

The slow, soft caresses and deep kisses. Pinning her to a wall and giving her the hard fucking she needed. And the talking—God, he loved talking to that woman. Her mind was an oyster opening to reveal a pearl, and he was damn well going to learn everything there was to know about her.

Their *maman's* footsteps sounded, and Lexi shoved him toward the stairs. "Go!"

He managed to reach the top floor and the bathroom he'd shared with his brothers growing up without explaining his appearance to his mother. After a hot shower and a good scrubbing, he felt semi-human. A clean set of clothes and he was ready to face anything, even on an empty stomach.

Though the fragrances of gumbo wafted upstairs and had his stomach twisting into a knot. Maybe he could spare a few minutes to grab a bowl of his *maman's* specialty.

By the time he hit the kitchen, Lexi, his parents and several of his brothers were just filling their bowls.

His mother's eyes widened. "Sean, I didn't know you were here. When did you come?"

"About the same time Lexi said what the fuck."

Their father arched a brow at his sister and she gave Sean a flat, I'm-going-to-murder-you look.

Maman started to get up to fetch him a bowl, but he waved her back down. "I got it." He grabbed the bowl from the cupboard and took a seat around the table with his family. Chaz was sporting a new cut on his cheek.

Sean didn't recall him having any injuries after their last operation.

Scooping some gumbo into his bowl, Sean said, "How'd you get that cut?"

Chaz shook his head, but Dylan spoke up. "Three little letters, bro. DEA."

Sean sat back in his seat and eyed Chaz. "She's a hellion, is she?"

"Only when pissed off." Chaz shot him a look but then added, "We're through. Too clingy for my tastes. Besides, I think she's secretly jealous that I have a dick."

"Chaz!" *Maman* covered her mouth with a hand as Lexi's giggles filled the room. Their father hid his grin in his gumbo.

"I'll have to tell Tyler about this," Lexi said.

"That's the last thing we need." Chaz glanced around the table as if just realizing their youngest sister wasn't present. "Where is Miss Wildcat anyway?"

Lexi fixed her attention on her gumbo, and Sean knew something was up, but he wasn't about to probe into that snake pit that made up their sisterhood. For years the twins had been plotting against him and the rest of their brothers, and Sean was in too good of a mood to get bitten.

He filled his mouth with a spoonful of rich gumbo and groaned. The shrimp was perfectly cooked, and the spices were Mardi Gras in his mouth. "This is excellent, *Maman.*"

She dropped her hand from her mouth where it was still planted in shock from Chaz's revelation. "Thank you. But can we please refrain from bad language around the table? This should be a sacred spot."

Properly contrite, Chaz nodded, but his lips twitched. "Maybe we should discuss Sean's girlfriend."

Fucking great.

Everyone's gazes snapped to him. "You have a girlfriend?" Lexi asked.

Dylan's stare settled on Sean, and he suddenly wondered why the hell he hadn't stolen out of the house before anybody spotted him. He was far from ready for questions about Elise, especially when he had no clue where he stood with her.

"Not a girlfriend, in the sense you're thinking." *And hoping and praying.* Ever since Ben had hooked up with Dahlia, their *maman* had been on them to find someone to settle down with.

Sean went on, "I've only spent a bit of time with her." He sent Chaz a long look that said

146

Don't worry — I'll get you back. He'd only brought up Elise to get the focus off himself.

Lexi jumped on the wagon too, always eager to shift the topic from herself. "Tell us about her, Sean. I already know she's pretty."

He didn't look up from his bowl, just kept shoveling it in. "How do you know that?"

"Because you have great taste in women."

He leveled a look at her. "Why are you buttering me up? What trouble are you in?"

She glanced away.

"She's gorgeous." Dylan's statement had all eyes on him and a growl rising in Sean's throat. "Should I tell them how you shoved me off my own job in order to work with her on those messages?"

"Lexi, cover your ears," their mother snapped. "You know we aren't allowed to know what goes on in OFFSUS."

"Just for mentioning OFFSUS, we'll have to put you under house arrest." Sean spooned up more gumbo. "And maybe I just wanted to learn a new skill, Dylan."

He grunted but said nothing. Sean was still touchy that his brother had noticed how gorgeous Elise was.

Hell, even a blind man would. A single look could slay a man. Throw in her dark eyes and full pout and he was fully hard. Not to

147

mention all that warm honey-colored skin to put his hands on.

"When will you be bringing this woman around?" *Maman's* question ended his mental undressing of Elise.

He glanced at his siblings. "Uh, not yet." If ever.

Suddenly, Lexi pushed back from the table. "I've gotta run. I'm late."

"Late?" *Pére* echoed. "You're in a hurry to get to the flower shop at this time of day? What's the rush?"

Lexi's cheeks bloomed with color, and Sean and his brothers shared a groan.

"Hell, I knew it," Chaz said.

"Best grab some shovels," Dylan added.

"Who is it this time?" Sean asked.

Lexi rolled her eyes. "You guys just love to think the worst of me."

"Not the worst of *you* — of your boyfriends," Sean said.

"I'm a grown-ass woman and I can make my own decisions."

Sean stared at her until she shifted on her feet. "Just keep him away from your bank account and remind him you have four brothers with certain... skills." He emphasized the last word in a deadly tone.

She set a hand on her hip and cocked her head. Gearing up for a tirade. As a child, she'd had them all fighting to see who could make her quit crying, but Sean was made of tougher stuff now.

"Settle down, y'all," *Maman* said. "Lexi can take care of herself."

Sean didn't think *maman* sounded so convinced that she could handle her newest and probably stupidest bad boyfriend, but he respected their mother's effort to smooth things over.

He flicked a gaze to his sister. "Just remind him." He dug into his gumbo again, and Lexi issued an exaggerated groan before clearing her bowl and leaving the house.

As soon as she was out of the room, Dylan pushed away from the table too. "I'll follow her."

"You'll do no such thing," their mother cried.

"We're just looking out for her, *Maman*." He dropped a kiss to her cheek, cleared his own bowl and headed out to tail their little sister.

Maman and *Pére* exchanged a look. "These boys are never going to let Lexi grow up."

Their father looked okay with that prospect.

Sean smiled. "C'mon, we don't just watch over Lexi. We'll break the legs of all Tyler's boyfriends too." Both sisters had horrible taste in men, and Sean wasn't the only one who believed that. They'd seen them come home in tears far too many times.

Their father shook his head, staying out of it as usual, and gave his wife a soft smile. "They mean well, Ellietta."

Sean took in the exchange between his parents. For the first time in his life, he wondered how they'd made their relationship stand so strong for so many years. They still looked at each other with such love in their eyes.

He watched them a minute more.

Before meeting Elise, would he have wondered these things? Sure, he'd considered what it would be like to have someone who cared about his safe return instead of fucking the next guy in line the minute he stepped out the door. But after only a few days with Elise, he could only picture himself going home — to *her*.

He stood up and grabbed his empty bowl. "I'm off. Thanks for the delicious food, *Maman*."

"You be sure to bring that lady friend of yours home soon, you hear?"

His heart expanded as he dropped a kiss to her cheek. "I'll see what I can do."

* * * * *

Elise eyed the man leaning against the doorway of her apartment, her mind and body at war with each other.

"Can I come in, *cher?*" Damn if Sean's low, rumbled words didn't have her fingers twitching to rip off all her clothes. Then jump his bones.

His fiiiine bones.

Her brain told her to slam the door in his face and hope like crazy she never set eyes on Sean Knight again. Except he was undressing her with his eyes, peeling off her T-shirt and running shorts with slow flicks of his eyes she felt over every inch of her very silly, very ramped-up body.

"Please?"

A simple plea shouldn't have her pulse pounding, yet it did. She ran her tongue over her lower lip.

His gaze fixed on her lower lip, and he groaned. "Can I just...?" Not waiting for her agreement, he stepped inside. She moved back as he crowded close, but his just-showered scent, mingled with the man himself, had her longing to rush into his arms.

He closed the door.

And locked it.

Two bad things.

"Sean—"

A simple look from him, dark eyes piercing through her, cut off what she was about to say.

"For the record, I fucking hate your ex."

She jerked, torn from her dirty thoughts of stripping off his clothes, starting with that fitted shirt that molded itself to every muscle of his shoulders, arms and torso. "Uhh... What did he do to you?"

His lashes were stupidly long for a man's. Surely, that should give him a weak appearance, but somehow the lengths only added to his appeal. He swiped a hand through the air, dismissing her words.

"I'll handle Hawk. Right now, I need to handle you."

A squeak left her, and she choked it off midway. Great, now she sounded like she'd swallowed a chicken bone. She took another step back, and he followed her.

Stalked her, more like.

"Sean, wait."

He stopped, his expression solemn. "Is there something going on with you and your ex?"

"Absolutely not. I told you that. We're friends, and he's a little overprotective of me."

"A little?" He cocked a brow, which only added to his dastardly appearance and spiked her libido another notch.

"Let me handle my ex-husband. And you'll just have to trust me when I say we're friends and nothing more."

His lips twisted momentarily, as if he couldn't quite trust her words or the meaning behind them. But it didn't matter, right? He could damn well leave if he didn't believe her.

"Now don't get that look on your face, *cher*. I didn't come here to fight."

"What look? And what did you come here to do then?"

"First, I'm talking about that look that tells me you know five kinds of martial arts and can kick my ass out of your apartment if I push you. I don't plan on pushing you. Second… maybe I do." He closed the gap between them, his body heat scorching through her shorts and thin black T-shirt. When he lifted a hand to cup her cheek, she barely swallowed the moan he raised from her throat.

"I…" She swallowed past her suddenly parched tongue. "Actually, I know six kinds of martial arts."

He nodded, staring right into her eyes. "And a strong woman needs a strong man to make you remember how feminine you are."

Oh God… how was he digging so deep into her psyche? She *had* loved how he'd guided her so easily in the bedroom, made her forget to be in control, to let go and just feel.

He leaned so close that his warm breath washed over her face. "First, I'm going to seduce you with kisses… and not just on your mouth."

Her pussy squeezed hard at his words.

"Then," his lids hooded, "after I've made you come at least twice, I'm going to lick you clean."

A shiver ran through her.

"Right before I slide into your tight pussy."

She had no words. Hell, she hardly had a thought in her head, just vivid images of everything he'd told her he'd do to her.

He ran his tongue over his lips like a hungry wolf, and she couldn't stop herself from tracking the movement. She felt the action deep in her body.

He gripped her hip, swaying her into him, and continued to run his hand up her torso to cup her breast.

"Ahh." Her moan was positively embarrassing.

"I can take you right here, right now. This carpet looks soft enough." He flicked his tongue at the corner of her lips. "Or you can show me to your bedroom."

She shuddered at his heated words and the stroke of his thumb across her nipple. The point hardened, and a dark need coiled inside her.

"That's what I thought. This way?" He flicked a glance over her shoulder toward the hall leading to her room.

Struck dumb, she nodded.

He swooped in and claimed her mouth. His rough kiss stealing all resistance, if she'd ever had any. She parted her lips and he drove his tongue in, seeking, stroking. Then he picked her up. With her legs dangling over his arm, she felt light and delicate. With each step he took toward her room, her body hummed louder.

One more night with Sean wouldn't hurt. She could break things off afterward, tell him how different they were and how it was pointless to go on.

Except it was a lie—they had loads in common. Hell, just being able to talk to someone about what they'd done back at that inn was huge to her. Any man she'd date would be left in the dark.

He stepped into her bedroom and stopped dead. Glancing around, his eyes lit with surprise.

"It's a little girly. You'll feel out of place."

He blinked, shedding that dazed expression. He stepped into the room farther and laid her gently on the frilly duvet on her plush mattress. "You're full of surprises, aren't you, *cher?*"

Feeling a little exposed, she averted her gaze. But he braced his arms on each side of her body and stretched out atop her, his lips hovering over hers.

"God, I love everything about you." His words tumbled out, rough and rumbly but sweeter than anything he'd said yet.

Without waiting for a response, he captured her lips again. Slowly, drawing her in with small nibbles and teases of his tongue. When she didn't think she could stand another second of his torment, he angled his head and sank his tongue deep into her mouth.

Need blasted her, leaving her feeling hot and cold as if she'd just stepped on a landmine and didn't know which way to turn. But her body knew—she wrapped her arms around his neck and dragged him down as he tongue-fucked her mouth until she grew dizzy.

Hooking her heel around his back, she yanked their hips together. His hard cock dug into her pussy, and they shared a throaty moan. With each slant of his tongue across hers, her passion soared higher.

As their kiss spiraled out of control, he stripped off her top. Her breasts were free and her nipples aching for his touch. He didn't make her wait long—he rolled one nipple between his fingers and thumb. She arched upward, gasping as he pinched it harder than he ever had before.

Need made her pussy spasm, and she rocked her hips. "More," she whispered, the sound urgent in the stillness of her apartment.

Those dark eyes of his flashed as he pulled from the kiss. "Oh, you'll get more, love."

He bit her lower lip—a quick nip of pain that only heightened her awareness more. Then he kissed her throat, her collarbones and finally down to her breasts. Spattering pecks around each and finally sucking one hard bud into his mouth.

"Oh God!" She gripped the back of his head and held him there as he delivered the most exquisite torment her body had ever known. The soft strands of his hair slipped through her fingers.

He flattened his tongue, and holding her gaze, licked his way to her other nipple. When he captured it between his teeth, she cried out. No way could she hold still. She fumbled with his fly, the zipper and button no match for the wild need inside her.

She reached into his jeans and skimmed her fingers over his thick erection. She followed the path of each ridge up to his flared head.

"Fuck. I'll never hold out if you keep doing that." His words sounded like he'd guzzled whiskey — the entire bottle.

His reaction amped up hers, and she tore at his pants and boxers, shoving them down his hips and them gripping his hard ass. His cock settled at the V of her legs.

"Get these pants off me — now." Her demand had him rumbling out another chuckle. Damn, she loved when he did that. He had no idea that she'd replayed those moments of playful laughter over and over in her head since they'd come together the first time.

Now...

His rough beard struck her sensitive skin. He skated his cheek down her belly to her waistband and then using his jaw, dragged the fabric down. He caught the elastic of her sweats in his fingers and towed them down and off.

He stared down at her tiniest—most impractical—pair of panties she owned. Pink and lacy, completely uncomfortable. By wearing them, it looked as if she'd been anticipating a lover.

He arched a brow.

"It's laundry day."

"Umm-hmm." His eyes hooded as he looked at the panties barely clinging to her mound, the sides like floss around her hips. A devilish gleam hit his eyes. "How much do you love these?"

"I... I hate them actually. They ride up my crack."

The rumbling laughter was back, causing a bone-deep tremble inside her. She didn't even want to think about why she reacted so strongly to him.

It was lust. Simple lust.

His lips quirked up in that bad-boy smile that would melt a stronger woman than her, and she considered herself pretty hardened to men's ploys. She'd spent her entire career dealing with guys who thought because they could throw pretty compliments her way that she'd spread her legs for them. But Sean

Knight seemed to have that mastered with a single twitch of his lips.

Without warning, he dipped his head. His teeth grazed her hip and then she felt the string holding up her panties snap.

"Oh my God." Made dizzy by the erotic action, she clutched at his shoulders. He moved to her other hip and took care of that string as well.

Locking gazes with her, he slid down her body, parting her thighs to make room for his wide shoulders. She couldn't look away. He very deliberately flicked his tongue out and strummed her clit.

The warm, wet caress ripped a cry from her lips. Juices squeezed from her folds, and he groaned as he lapped them.

When he pressed his fingertips into her outer lips and parted her to make way for his tongue, her inner thighs quivered. Another gasping cry left her. This man knew how to pluck all the right chords.

He swirled his tongue around her nubbin with the skill of a professional gigolo. At this minute, she didn't care who he'd practiced on before her — she was thrilled with the benefits of having an experienced man who knew her body so well.

She bucked her hips, and he sank his tongue into her channel. Liquid heat moving in and out of her stole all thought until he pressed his callused thumb into her clit.

Her nerves went haywire, and the tight knot in her lower belly shredded into oblivion. Her orgasm struck with a force she couldn't think through. The first pulsation slammed her, and she was helpless to do anything but scream Sean's name.

Dammit, she'd just fed his ego.

* * * * *

Sean's grin stretched as he continued to bathe Elise's pussy with his lips and tongue, tasting her release even as his eardrums vibrated with it. He had to admit he was damn pleased she'd called out his name. It felt like a victory.

It wasn't about making a conquest—it was about knowing she was feeling the same things he was.

As her final pulsations faded away, he delivered one last slow lick from the bottom of her pussy to the top, gathering the last drops of her release.

She shuddered beneath him, her fists twisting the ruffled covers of her bed. That too had been a surprise, and he knew there was so much more to Elise than she wanted people to see.

But he was here to tell her—with his teeth and tongue if necessary—that she couldn't conceal anything from him.

A final shudder left her, and she went boneless. Grinning, he moved up her body, kissing a trail to her lips. When he probed the corner of her mouth, she twisted into the caress with a gasp of desperation.

His heart somersaulted and kept rolling. She poked her tongue into his mouth and kissed him greedily.

He growled and cupped her head in one palm, drinking from her long and deep even as he realized his heart wasn't going to recover.

He was a goner.

He couldn't catch his breath and didn't care if he ever did again. If she made him feel this excited, breathless and out of control, then he was officially an addict.

He flipped onto his back, settling her on top of him. Her sexy curves plastered to his body was something he couldn't get enough of. That left only one answer to his dilemma— he had to make sure he kept her happy so she never left his bed.

With a shimmy of her hips, she had his cock nearly bursting. He groaned and stilled

162

her. But she refused to remain in place and eased down his body with a private smile and a glitter in her eyes that told him he was in... so... much... trouble.

"Elise," he rasped when her lips hit his abs and skittered down into the short tangle of hairs cushioning his cock. She mouthed the root of his shaft, and he damn near lost it there and then.

He felt the veins in his neck bulge with the effort of retaining his control as she slid her mouth along his cock to the tip. Her warm breath enveloped him for a split second before she swallowed him.

"Jesus Christ."

She made a noise that could have been a giggle and did something with her tongue that had his hips coming off the bed. Hell, at this rate, he'd be glued to the ceiling. The woman knew how to give head.

He couldn't drag in air around the groan he was releasing. Speaking of releasing...

Pre-cum leaked onto her scorching-hot tongue and he had no idea if he was going to stave off his impending orgasm.

"Stop." He gripped her shoulders and yanked her up.

Her smile spread across her beautiful features, and he couldn't stop staring at her. Or at her ripe lips swollen from sucking his cock.

"I'm going to finish you off," she said.

"I'll take you up on that. But not today. Reach over the side and grab a condom from my wallet, would you?"

"I'll do better than that." She leaned forward and opened her nightstand drawer.

His eyes bulged when he saw the number of condoms there. "Please tell me you don't have those for anyone besides me."

She just gave him a small smile and ripped open a packet. He was mesmerized by her fingers as she rolled the rubber over his cock. Then she arched her back, thrusting her breasts forward.

He caught them in his palms and swished his thumbs over her distended nipples as she poised her pussy over his erection.

"Slide down on me, *cher*. Take what you want."

Her eyelids fluttered as she eased down over him inch by slick inch. Heat spread through his groin, and his balls tightened. He kneaded her breasts and jerked his hips upward, his cock buried so deep that he couldn't think of where his body separated from hers.

Then she started to move. Slowly at first, with small rolls of her hips. Each movement growing faster, more and more out of control, until her throaty moans echoed off the flowery wallpapered walls. He grabbed her hips and guided her, up and down, faster until she let out a scream that hit him like an air strike.

His orgasm rushed up and overflowed, jets spurting from him rapid-fire.

"Oh my God," she whispered and collapsed on his chest.

Her silky hair spread across his chest, and some of it caught on the stubble of his jaw. He didn't move. Couldn't move. And she seemed content to lie there and recover.

Stroking his fingers up and down her spine raised goosebumps in his wake, and damn if he didn't feel good about that too. He loved how reactive she was to his touch.

After long minutes, she eased off him, mindful of the condom that had to be about to burst from all the cum he'd shot into it. She rolled onto the mattress and he leaned over to brush his lips over hers. "I'll just take care of this."

He got up and went to the first door off her bedroom. Her giggle followed him. "That's the closet."

He grabbed the first lacy thing he saw hanging and came out dangling it on one finger. "You should put this on."

She laughed again and shook her head. He set aside the lacy dress and then found the bathroom. It only took him a minute to clean up—he wasn't wasting a minute of his time with her. Especially when he had no idea when he'd be called out to duty again.

He emerged from the bathroom to find her sitting up, the blankets tucked under her armpits. Her dark hair tumbled over one sexy shoulder.

"Damn, you look fine." He ran the few steps to the bed and dived onto the mattress, making her giggle and bounce into his arms. He drew her against him and she flipped the ruffled covers over his shoulder.

Another laugh escaped her. He stared at her.

"What?"

"I've never seen you so carefree," he said, in awe.

"Well, I've never seen a man wear ruffles so well. I don't know how, but you look even more manly."

He cocked a brow and gave her a crooked smile. "It's the tattoo, isn't it?"

Her gaze flicked down to the eagle clutching a rippling flag in its talons inked across his chest. She nodded. "I think it is." She raised a hand to the tattoo and just her soft touch against his skin had him hard again.

The covers tented around his erection, and she tugged the blanket back to peek. "Seems we have a problem, Knight."

"Mmm. I can see a couple myself." He stroked her hardened nipple through the sheet.

Her eyes grew serious as she stared at him. "First, you have to promise that if you get called away for a mission while I'm asleep that you'll wake me and tell me."

His heart gave a hard thud of emotion at her words. Leaning in, he pressed his forehead against hers, breathing in her sweetness. "Promise. But you'd better not be the type of woman who wakes from a sound sleep swinging a fist."

She chuckled but looked a bit worried. "Who does that?"

"My sister Tyler."

"Oh yes, I've heard of her."

His brows shot up. "Tell me it's not because she's dating some jarhead."

"You don't want her with a Marine?"

"Not if I can help it. I've known too many Marines." His mind went to Elise's ex and how a man like Hawk would never, ever lay hands on his sister. Because Sean would take pure pleasure into smashing each digit into bone pulp.

"What does that say about you?" Elise asked.

"I'm different. Ask anyone."

"Hmm." She didn't sound so convinced, and there was only one way to get her off the topic. He lowered his head and kissed her with a slow intensity that left them both gasping. He skimmed a hand over her bare hip, up to her narrow waist. Things quickly heated, and in minutes, he was sporting another condom and thrusting his cock high and deep into her tight pussy.

Looking down into her eyes, he said, "I'm good for you. Tell me you don't feel it."

She closed her eyes and let out a rasp of pleasure.

He grinned. "I'll take that."

Chapter Seven

The breeze rippled through the trees, making the Spanish moss sway on the branches and stirring memories in Elise. She shifted on the edge of the dock, feet swaying, and one bare toe swished the water, causing ripples. Each ring spread out wider and wider until they enveloped her and Sean's fishing lines.

"What's that sigh for?" His deep voice bathed over her. She couldn't decide if his presence or the sun on her shoulders made her feel warmer.

She looked to him. "Did I sigh?"

His smile spread over his ruggedly handsome features. His beard had sprouted even more in the Louisiana humidity and now couldn't be called stubble. It was definitely the beginnings of a yummy beard.

"Yes, you sighed. Are you frustrated we're not catching any catfish?"

When he'd asked her to come with him for an afternoon of fishing, she had jumped at the chance. "That's not it. I learned patience in this hobby."

169

He dropped his jaw. "Hobby? This is a sport, *cher.*"

She chuckled. "That's what my grandpére would say. I was thinking of him when I sighed, actually."

While working such long hours together, she'd discovered one of the things she liked most about Sean was how he could sit so still and quietly, waiting for her to say what was on her mind. Totally the opposite of Bo, who wanted to know and wanted to know now. She'd gotten used to Bo's ways, but she had to admit she preferred Sean's.

"My grandfather used to bring me catfishin' as a little girl."

"He's gone now?" he asked softly.

"Yes. Four years ago. He was a great man in my life. The only man, since my father ran out on us. The old, I'm-going-to-the-store-for-cigarettes trick." She gave Sean a sideways glance.

"Damn, that's harsh. The least he could do was come up with something original."

That brought a laugh from her, so unexpected and genuine that she warmed toward him more. He put his arm around her, one hand still gripping the pole. They were more likely to get a hundred mosquito bites out here than a catfish, but she didn't want to spoil the mood by telling him he was going at it all wrong. Just sitting on the dock with him felt nice.

Actually, it felt like a departure from her life and a trip back in time all at once.

His intense gaze fixed on her. "Can I ask you about your roots? I'm curious what flavors went into making such a beautiful woman."

A hot flush climbed her cheeks. Men called her beautiful, sure. And more than one Marine had tried to get in her pants. But when Sean complimented her, she felt it deep in a part of her that had never been touched before, not even when Bo had told her when she'd walked down the aisle.

"I have the typical Creole on my father's side and if you're wondering if I have a voodoo priestess in my family tree, you're correct."

His brows shot up.

She nodded. "Great grandmére. My mother remembers sitting with her and hearing her curse people under her breath." She giggled, and they shared a laugh.

"So that's where you get your demeanor."

She shoved at his shoulder, hoping he fell into the water, but he didn't even rock. "What's that supposed to mean?"

"I don't have to tell you that you're tough and ruthless if need be."

Now his compliment gave her a new sensation. She'd always prided herself on her abilities, whether it was the mental dismantling of codes nobody was supposed to crack or hand-to-hand combat. The fact that Sean saw her so clearly gave her a thrill.

"Maybe you're right."

"And your *maman*?"

"Moved to Florida."

"You don't sound happy about that."

"I always felt she..." She paused, unsure whether she should voice something she'd never admitted aloud to anybody. "Is it terrible I thought her weak for wanting to run away and never getting over my father leaving?"

He shook his head. "Your feelings are valid, whatever they are, *cher*."

She dragged in a deep breath and released it, considering his words. "She needed a fresh start, and after I joined the forces, she got it. She's living with a man quite happily these past few years."

"That's good then."

She looked into Sean's eyes, seeing more about her own life through his vision. "Yeah," she said, surprised, "it is." Until then, she'd always wondered if her mother's choices had been the right ones, but it was obvious they were. Anything that gave a person happiness was worth fighting for.

"I'm sorry about the men in your life, Elise."

She held her breath, hearing what he wasn't saying about the men in her life. He was so curious about Bo, and if she was sleeping with him—and she most definitely had many times—he deserved to know.

She inclined her head toward his line. "You're not going to catch a catfish on that bait."

He chuckled. "I know. You may not know this about me, but I'm the king of catfishin'. I can pull more out of the water in an hour than you or I would want to deal with. This way we get a chance to talk, get to know each other." He leaned in to brush his lips over her cheekbone.

She turned her mouth into his, the kiss sweet and lingering. A boy meets girl kind of kiss, from a romantic movie where the couple figures out they actually might have a future together.

Except, she wasn't snowing herself over by thinking she and Sean would end up together. More than likely, she'd have another Bo in her life—a buddy. But as soon as she tried to take that step toward a real relationship, she'd

173

realize what she had about Bo—that they weren't suited. Maybe she wasn't suited to settling down with anybody, but she was fine with that.

He drew back from the kiss, eyes warm and bright, melting her insides. "I love being with you, Elise."

"I..." A private smile stretched her lips. "I'm glad we came here."

"You're glad you came. And came. And came. And came. And—"

"All right." She laughed and nudged his shoulder with hers. "I'm glad we did that too."

He cracked a smile that was a portrait of cockiness if she ever saw one. But he didn't need her to tell him that he was a great lover. The man knew his skills in bed and in the field.

"Sean." She spoke hesitantly.

His expression grew serious. "What is it?"

"I know you want to know more about Bo."

She saw the change come over him.

"I admit I'm curious about your odd relationship."

"Odd?"

"Surely you must know most divorced people aren't best friends after the split-up."

She nodded, chewing her lip a bit. "Yes. It's just that we were way better friends than we ever were anything else. We just didn't realize it until we'd tried the other path."

He nodded as if he understood, but she wondered if he really did.

"You don't have anything to be jealous over, Sean. Bo and I… we were through before we started. We mistook a deep bond of friendship and a working relationship for love. He is invested in what happens to me, and I am too."

"You interfere in who he sees?"

"No, not that. In fact, I don't want to know anything about his conquests. But he's there for me in any way I need him."

Sean issued a low sound in his throat that had her leaning close to catch his gaze. He slid his stare to hers. "I don't like it."

"Why not? I already told you he's not a love interest."

"Because I want to be there for you in any way you need, and he can keep his interfering ass out of it."

Excitement speared her, a hot spike through her heart and into her core. His words roused something she hadn't considered when first jumping into the sack with Sean. The idea that he might get attached, want more... No, she must be misreading what he was saying.

A man like Sean Knight couldn't be telling her that he wanted to be there for her in all ways, like a man who loved a woman was. Sean was too tough for such emotions.

And so was she.

* * * * *

The banging on the front door followed by a string of dings from Elise's phone could only mean one person had come to visit.

"Bo," she groaned.

Next to her, Sean bolted upright. His hair stood out in several directions and the stubble on his jaw had gone from dangerous to dastardly.

"Tell me that fucker's not at your door right now," he grated out. He jumped out of bed, looking about to reach for his weapon and clear the perimeter.

She glanced at the clock. 1:00 a.m. She scrambled to her feet and grabbed for her robe as she circled the bed. The place looked like a war zone, with clothes and shoes strewn across the pale carpet. He jerked on his jeans.

"Sean, hold on." She pressed a hand to his chest. His heart was racing — an adrenaline rush. Nobody liked being woken from a deep

176

sleep let alone with such alarming urgency. Bo beat at the door again, and her phone rang with several more text messages.

She snatched it off the nightstand and looked up into Sean's eyes. "Let me handle Bo."

"Like hell." He started to move around her, and she stepped into his path.

"No, really. I got this."

"What could be so urgent that he has to do that?" He pointed at the front of the apartment as more pounding ensued.

Bo called out, "Elise! Open the door. Now."

Sean's mouth hardened, and she saw the steel in his demeanor—what made him a warrior—or maybe a Knight. He pushed past her and strode into the living room. She ran out and jumped between him and the door.

"Sean, I'll handle this. Just… go make a pot of coffee."

"He's not fucking ordering you around." He didn't look at her as he said this, just glared at the door as if he could drill through the wood and into the man on the other side.

At her back, the door vibrated with Bo's extreme pounding. If he kept this up, he would get her kicked out of the apartment building.

Sean reached for the handle, and she gripped his wrist. Raising the other hand, she cupped his jaw. He must have seen the determination on her face to win this round because he stepped back.

"Fine. But I'm not leaving you alone with him."

She gritted her teeth. Having two alpha males vying for her attention—even for different reasons—was not up there on her comfort scale.

And now she was going to have to deal with Bo walking in to see Sean wearing only his jeans and her in a state of dishevelment that could only mean she'd been pleasured well into the night.

She took a breath and opened the door.

Bo pinned her in his stare and dropped the fist he had poised to beat down her door again. "What took you so long?" He stepped past her and stopped dead as he and Sean faced off.

Oh fuck.

She couldn't let them fight. This was stupid and there was no reason for either of them to have a problem. If she was going to keep Sean in her life, she needed them to come to this conclusion.

"I fucking knew it." Bo's tone came out in that flat way that she knew all too well. She'd heard it enough on operations. It was his I'm-going-to-make-you-wish-you-weren't-born tone.

Sean cocked a brow. "What the fuck do you need, Hawk?"

"It's not a cup of coffee. I need Elise."

A vein bulged in Sean's temple.

Elise got between them. "Guys, take it easy, okay?"

Part of her realized whatever Bo had come here for was urgent. He wouldn't be blowing up her phone and tearing down her door if it weren't.

Behind her, the door opened again and she heard a deep chuckle that made her whirl. She made a grab for the front of her robe, hoping no skin was showing because the entire Knight Ops team had shown up.

They were standing in her living room, assessing the situation.

Great—now she'd officially met Sean's brothers in her slinky robe sporting his beard burn on her throat and the tops of her breasts.

"What is it?" Sean asked them in that no-nonsense tone that rivaled Bo's.

His brother Ben gave him a once-over. "You had your phone turned off."

"Yeah, so?"

Elise's eyes widened. He'd silenced his phone, ignored his duty just to spend a night with her uninterrupted?

Ben twitched his head toward the door. "We're ready to roll. We've got all the zip-ties you need."

A low growl came from Bo, and Sean jerked his head to pierce him in his gaze. The pair glared at each other for five full heartbeats before Elise took action.

"Okay, Sean, duty calls. Bo, can I speak with you in the kitchen?"

"The Knight Ops need to hear this too." Concern pinched Bo's brows. Her heart rate picked up.

"What the fuck's going on, Hawk?" Sean demanded, fists clenched.

"Elise has been made. I need to get her out of here."

"M-made?" She stumbled over the word.

"When you downloaded those messages— somehow they found you. I need you to come with me."

"Just a damn minute." Sean stepped up to Bo. They were matched in height and muscle, but Sean looked angrier, more capable of bodily harm. "You're going to take Elise away and protect her?"

He gave a sharp nod.

The tattoos covering Sean's shoulder and arm seemed to ripple, and she realized his muscles were so tense they were quivering.

"Thunder, we need you dressed and outside in two minutes." Ben's order made Sean blink but that was all. The man was a hard-ass, that was for sure. As well as reckless.

"Sean, you've got to go. I'll be okay."

He ignored her and directed his question at her ex. "Where are you taking her?"

"That's confidential. But she'll be safe."

"Thunder, the clock's ticking."

He swung his gaze to his brother. "Give me three." Then he caught Elise's hand and dragged her to the bedroom, slamming the door behind him.

They stared at each other.

He let out an uneven sigh. "Jesus Christ, Elise. I need to stay and protect you."

She was shaking her head before he completed the sentence. "You have a duty, and I'll be fine. I'm not helpless, you know."

His jaw tensed, and his eyes glittered with some emotion she couldn't name. Suddenly, he jammed his fingers through his hair, sending it into wild spikes. "Dammit, I should be guarding your life."

"Bo's done it before."

His eyes bulged. Maybe that was the wrong thing to say.

"I'll be fine, I promise. Now get dressed and get out there. Your team needs you." She picked up his shirt and tossed it to him.

He caught it one-handedly and stepped forward to slide an arm around her back, dragging her against his hard body. For a moment, she couldn't think or breathe. Fear for what was to come—for them both—was too close to the surface.

He dropped his nose to her hair and inhaled. "I don't know when I'll be back."

Because he had no idea where he was going. She understood that—it was part of the lifestyle. Hell, she didn't know where she was headed or when she'd return either. If she was lucky, they'd shake off the threat hanging over her and she could stay out of witness protection. She didn't relish the idea of changing her appearance and identity.

Behind them, the door flew open. Sean shielded her with his body, and Bo's face turned purple with anger.

Sean released her and gently pushed her behind him as he turned to face her ex. There was so much testosterone in her bedroom that the ruffles would melt, she was sure of it.

She placed a hand on Sean's shoulder and peered around him. Bo slashed a look at her.

Sean made a low noise in his throat. "I'm guessing my operation is connected to Elise being made. As much as I want to be in two places at once, I can't. So I'm putting her in your hands and trusting that you will keep her safe."

Her jaw dropped.

Bo rocked on his boots, the slightest movement which told her that he was as surprised as she was to hear those words come from Sean's mouth.

"I give my word to guard her life."

She wanted to chime in and tell them she was capable of keeping herself alive, but she didn't want to squash their man moment. It might not be bonding, but it was the closest they'd come to a truce.

Sean gave a hard nod and then said, "Get out. I need a minute with her."

Bo avoided her gaze as he went out of the room and closed the door behind him. They were well past the three minutes Sean had asked for, but he didn't appear concerned.

His eyes softened as he looked down at her. She threw her arms around his neck, going on tiptoe and molding her body to his. In their business, they never knew which moment would be their last, and she'd long ago learned to make every one count when it came to relationships.

Is that what they had? A relationship? It felt like a beginning.

He lowered his head and kissed her, a soft brushing of his mouth that left her aching—in her heart as well as her body. Deep stirrings in her core had her longing for his big thigh wedged between her legs so she could rock her—

Letting out a shaky sigh, she stepped back.

"I'll come find you after. Don't take any unnecessary risks, love." His words tightened her throat.

She nodded. "You either."

He tugged on his shirt with that crooked smile she was growing to need like a junkie needed meth. "I'll be fine, I swear."

She knew he couldn't make promises like that, but she appreciated the words anyway. She watched him dress and tie his boots. Then he pressed another hard kiss to her lips before throwing open the door.

Bo stood there waiting.

"I'm trusting you, Hawk. Don't fuck this up," he said and strode out of her apartment. But hopefully not her life.

*****

"Goddammit." Sean glared at the side mirror of the Knights Ops vehicle until Elise's apartment building faded from view. Then he jammed the heel of his hand on the dashboard.

Ben pushed out air through his nostrils. "We need you focused, Sean. Get your shit together because you play a bigger role in this than what you know."

That jerked his head around. He looked at his brother, who didn't appear to be in much better condition than him. Damn, was this what love did to a man?

His brain tripped over the word — love. Did he love Elise?

"What the hell are you talking about?" he demanded of his brother.

"The Russian's back on the radar, and Jackson's given you an opportunity."

The SUV was completely silent.

His heart slammed his chest well. "Opportunity?"

"Yeah, we're joining forces with another OFFSUS team that just lost their leader."

Of course they weren't the only team in Operation Freedom Flag in the South, but any one of those leaders would mean a huge loss to the world.

185

He swallowed hard. Lost could mean anything, but in their line of work, it didn't often mean that the operator had put in for vacation.

Sean fisted his hands on his knees. "Dammit, don't tell me who. I'm not in the mood."

This was piss-poor timing. The one thing he'd been striving to achieve for the past few years — a team leader role — was now within his grasp.

Leading his own unit. And not any platoon but a fucking OFFSUS special ops team. A chance to make a difference, and not as someone's sidekick.

Fuck. Getting what he wanted came with higher stakes than he would have imagined. Leaving Elise in the hands of her ex-husband had almost killed him. And he was about to lose it if he even thought about Hawkeye not living up to his reputation when it came to skill. If one hair on Elise's pretty little head got yanked out, so help him —

Ben braked hard, and tires squealed. Sean was ripped from his thoughts as he spotted the other black SUV sitting alongside the road, nearly undetected in the darkness.

"This is you. Good luck, Sean." Ben's expression broadcast so much more than his words.

"Tell me this isn't the Pee-Wees."

"It isn't."

"What the hell happens to you guys?" Sean twisted in his seat to look at Dylan, Chaz, Roades and Rocko. "You're short-handed."

Rocko tipped his jaw at Sean. "We're picking up one of my former teammates. We'll see you there, Thunder."

What else was there to say or do? Sean nodded at each of his team before climbing out of the vehicle. When he got into the passenger's seat of the other SUV, five men greeted him.

His men.

Fuck.

He had one chance and he couldn't blow it, but for the next mile they drove, all he could think about was Knight Ops and Elise. He felt as if his guts were being torn out.

Where was she right now? Fleeing with Bo to some safehouse? Sean hadn't even gotten to say a proper goodbye—not the way he wanted to. He'd planned to take his leave from her slowly in the morning, to wake her with coffee and a hot shower, where he'd slide his soapy fingers all over her curves and finally brace her against the wall and fuck her.

All those hopes had popped like a bubble, and now she was on the run and he was facing God knew what.

"Sean Knight," he said at last to his new team.

"Frisco, Cap'n." The driver tossed him a grin. He bore a jagged scar up his bare arm that disappeared under the sleeve he'd ripped off his shirt. It was still red, freshly healed. These guys had stories just like theirs.

The others called out their names. McMahon, Corporon, Depeux and Wolf. All of them good old Southerners just like the Knight Ops team.

He gave a light shake of his head. "Y'all sound like a bunch of bayou boys. I guess when they organized the Southern division, they took it seriously."

A light cheer went up, and Frisco shot him an amused glance. "That's right. We're glad you're leading us, Cap'n."

An odd sting of pride in his chest caught Sean off guard. It welled into a burn, and he resisted the urge to rub a hand over the spot. Damn, what he wouldn't give to tell Elise about this.

But she was gone from him for now. *That motherfucker Hawk better take good care of her.*

Frisco made a quick right turn onto a back road Sean knew as a cutoff.

"Tell me we're not going where I think we're going," he said to Frisco.

McMahon made a few twangy noises that mimicked a banjo and the others hummed a bar of an old Cajun tune about a swamp monster. But that's what this team was—each one of them capable of sneaking in and out where only a paranormal creature would roam.

"You said it, Knight. They picked us Southern boys for a reason." Frisco's teeth flashed white. "Swamp rats, every one of us. Welcome to Team *Rougarou*. We're supposed to go in and flush these Russkies out while Knight Ops captures them."

Until this moment, the team he was now leading was only rumored to be real. Named after a mythical werewolf living in the swamps, it was no wonder nobody knew the truth.

Sean looked out the windshield. Russkies? More than one Russian? "Fuck."

His response was met by laughter and a cheer. "We save the fucking for later, Cap'n. Always got women eager to celebrate our victories."

Sean grinned. "Then let's get this done fast so we can get to the ladies." Visions of Elise brought him down to earth again. He was going to tear Hawk apart if she wasn't safe.

"What's the strategy, Knight?" There had to be a reason behind Frisco's nickname, because the man had the most Cajun accent Sean had ever heard, but now wasn't the time for getting to know his men. That could come after they did their jobs.

Sean's brain worked over the little information he had. At least he knew these swamps like he knew the curves of Elise's body.

Damn, he really had it bad for that woman.

He cleared his throat. "Get ready, boys. I've got an idea."

* * * * *

Sean made a hand-chopping motion toward the west. "I think they're hunkered down there. It's the thickest cover in fucking Louisiana. Two of us circle around and get in a position behind them while Depeux, you provide some cover shots. That should lure them out and get them riled up, especially when Wolf sends some shots over their heads from the east."

190

The group of men nodded at his command.

His earpiece cracked as it came to life, Ben's voice filling his ear. "We're in position."

"Copy that." Sean didn't like the thought of his brothers and Rocko and another Navy turned OFFSUS man named Gallagher being on that side of the war without him. But he had a job to do.

He nodded at McMahon. "You're with me. Corporon, you move between Depeux and Frisco, make sure they're covered."

"Got their backs, boss man." Corporon's deep baritone could easily fit into a backwoods jug band—it had a musical quality in his singsong way of speaking.

"Heading out," he said to Ben.

"Good luck."

"Guts and glory, bro," came Dylan's voice.

"Guts and glory," Sean returned, throat thick.

For the next five minutes, they spread out, he and McMahon picking their way through cover so thick, they could barely see in front of them. With their night goggles, they had enough vision to pick out the spaces between brambles and tangled vines for places to slip through. Sweat poured down Sean's neck and into the collar of his shirt. What he wouldn't give for that shower with Elise right now.

Putting her from his mind, he focused on his senses. He had to stay alive to find her again.

First, the Russian. Or Russians. Apparently, the guy had brought friends. No matter, because Team Rougarou and Knight Ops would make short work of them. They wouldn't be happy to find themselves surrounded in Manchac Swamp.

This time Sean was packing more than zip-ties.

Captured once, shame on you. Captured twice, you're dead.

He pressed his lips into a line and motioned for McMahon to set up. He could practically hear heartbeats in the center of the small patch of land they had surrounded. He listened harder. Not voices, exactly, but a whisper of wind, slightly off-rhythm.

Maybe he really did belong with Team Rou. He relied on mystical shit just as much as they did, it seemed.

A whiff of smoke hit his nostrils, and McMahon's head shot up. "You're fucking kidding me. What asshole smokes those cheap fucking cigars?" McMahon drawled.

192

Sean flashed him an amused glance. "Dumb fuckers who have access to American garbage."

"Well, I'll give him something good to smoke right before I hand him over."

They bumped knuckles and then settled down to make their move.

Minutes passed with a volley of talk, chatter coming from the other guys in Rou, teasing and ribbing that rivaled what the Knight Ops crew did in these situations.

Sean went still. Knight Ops. Why hadn't Ben spoken up in the past twenty minutes? He had to be in position by now, ready for Sean and his men to flush out these fuckers so they could capture them.

"Thunder to Knight One."

The silence that came back at him had his heart thumping wildly.

"Fuck, Knight Ops isn't where they need to be. What's wrong with these city boys?"

"Watch it, Depeux," Sean snapped. "Something's the matter. Ben, Dylan, state your positions."

A crackle in his ear had Sean's spine straightening. But when a shot fired that didn't come from the direction of Depeux or Frisco, he rocketed to his feet. McMahon jumped up too.

193

Sean's mind worked the situation in a blink, and he unraveled the dilemma into a clear objective. As usual, things had gone sideways, and for some reason, Knight Ops was not able to get into position. Probably because they were now taking fire from a second group of Russians holed up on the opposite side of their position.

Sean saw only one chance to get these assholes, and he wasn't going to lose it. He threw McMahon a look. "We're not pushing these Russkies out, McMahon—we're going in. On three."

Chapter Eight

Elise gazed at the computer screen in front of her. Never in a million years would she believe she'd be cracking codes that led back to herself. But the war she was fighting was one of genius minds, and she had to fight fire with fire. It was the only way to nail these people who were after her. She needed to get ahead of them, to know what path they'd take to find her.

Bo had set her up in a cabin on the edge of nowhere, and it was far from a vacationer's dream setting. Hell, the abandoned restaurant where she'd started out with Dylan and Sean was better than this.

Of course, in her mind, nothing could compare to the inn where she and Sean had finally blown open the whole case. There, she'd seen just how brilliant his mind was, how he could keep up to her in every way.

Crap, she had to put him out of her head. Who knew when they'd see each other again. Bo refused to tell her anything about Knight Ops' operation.

Her fingers ached, and she realized she was gripping the edge of the table so hard her fingertips were white. She pulled her hands back and rubbed at a splinter embedded too deep to pick out without a needle.

Things sometimes went wrong on missions. Like when she'd downloaded the files, which had drawn a fat red X over her location the minute she'd opened them. She'd moved around enough to throw off the people trying to locate her, but eventually they'd pinned her down at her apartment.

Whoever had written that little program into the secret messages was a fucking Einstein. She was good at what she did, but she couldn't begin to wrap her head around the methods used to find her.

But now she was turning the tables on the sonofabitches—she would not be found. Nope, she planned to live her life without fear and worry that she and Sean would be—

She cut off that thought.

Pushing out a breath, she drifted to the window. It seemed more and more when thinking about the man who'd rocked her world since demanding his place in it, she'd stand at this grubby window and look out on... well, nothing. Trees surrounded her, branches so thick she could hardly make out a bird.

At the click of the door lock, she turned to see Bo entering the space, dressed in all black, his face smudged with black streaks so only the whites of his eyes stood out and his teeth if he saw fit to smile.

He dropped his gaze over her, and she stared back. "You haven't finished, have you?"

"No."

"Jesus, Elise. I've never seen you this way." He put his back to the door, a human barrier. She'd like to see who could get through her ex, though Sean had, hadn't he? He'd shimmied into her life right under Bo's nose.

She wet her dry lips and walked back to the computer. "What way?"

"You're afraid. I've seen you take on four men at once without a blink of fear. You've dropped into enemy territory just to get intel and you never faltered. But this…"

She sank to the chair and avoided his gaze, though she did wonder where he was going with this walk down the Marines memory lane.

She cocked a brow.

He came to stand in front of her. "You're afraid," he said again.

Considering his words only left her confused as to how she felt. "I'm cautious, not afraid. Anybody would be stupid to underestimate the people looking for me."

197

He grunted. "I'm not talking about that, Elise. You're afraid you're not going to see Sean again."

At his name, her heart gave a wild lurch. Her ears pounded with the jump in her heart rate. "What do you know about Sean?"

Bo stared at her, his dark eyes unwavering. "Holy hell. You're in love with him."

Her brows pinched, and she shook her head.

He nodded. "Oh yes, you are. No wonder I've never seen you this way before, Elise. I've never seen you in love."

Her jaw dropped on a quiver of a sigh as pain and guilt bled through her chest. He was right—she'd never loved Bo the way a wife was supposed to love a husband, and she'd always felt like the lowliest scum because of it. What woman couldn't love Bo that way? He was damned amazing. Hell, he even loved to go clothes shopping.

But her heart told her it wasn't right, and so had his.

"Bo, I'm—"

He made a slashing motion in the air with one hand. "Don't apologize, Elise. This isn't about us."

She blinked. "It isn't?"

He shook his head. "You're in love with Sean Knight. Jesus Christ."

She blinked. Love? Was she in love with him? Confusion tore at her, digging its claws deep until she looked up at Bo for help.

"Sweetheart, you're worried about the man. You're sitting here pining for him. And I've never seen you wear that glow you wore when you both came out of your bedroom." He sounded more amused than shocked, and she grasped that with both hands.

Right now, as usual, they were not people who'd once been bound by matrimony. They were the closest of friends.

"You think?"

"I *know*. Think about it, Elise."

She pivoted in her seat to the window again, blasted by a need to set eyes on Sean and make sure he was safe. To touch him, to feel his kisses, his caresses, his cock moving deep inside her...

Standing, she put her hands on Bo's shoulders and looked into his eyes. An urgency fired her blood. "I need to know where he is, and you can tell me."

He drew his lips tight across his teeth. After a full minute, he released a sigh. "The man's worthy, at least."

"Bo."

"He fucking tied me up with zip-ties and left me back in that swamp. You know that, right?"

She nodded, a sudden temptation to giggle teasing her lips. She bit it back.

"And he's just led Rou to capture that spy who'd been in the wind and in the process, located the people behind those missing warheads. It's fucking huge."

The information rolled over her, and her mind clung to one small detail. Team Rou was another special ops unit in OFFSUS, a group of guys known for getting into tight spots and being ruthless in their activities.

Her mouth dried out. "*Rougarou?*"

"Yeah, named after the Cajun werewolf said to prowl the Manchac Swamp."

"I know what it is," she said.

"They're as wild as their name claims, trackers and hunters from the bayou, all of them dirty players willing to take risks most aren't." He eyed her, and since he was a true swamp rat himself, she saw the same wildness in his eyes. "And Knight's being given leadership."

She was nodding, but her heart was beating too fast. "I know them."

His gaze penetrated her. "Of course you do. You're in the middle of everything. I hope to hell Knight knows how to handle that. It's damn nerve-wracking." Bo trailed off on a mutter.

She squeezed his arm. "What are you talking about, handling that? Handling me? Are you stepping aside as my handler?" Her heart gave a small lurch of heartbreak even as it swelled at the idea of Sean working so closely with her. Their chances of being caught with their clothes off might be increased by about a million times, though.

Bo took her hand. "I'm not walking away from anything. You're an important asset to us, Elise, and you're important to me. From what I see coming, Sean will be leading his own unit after this."

Her heart dropped. Any man could fall when it came to being a special operative, but the leader was usually the man who took the hit if it meant saving the others. Sean would be even more of a target. Could she handle living that way?

The revelation hit like a hurricane wind, shaking her to her bones. Yes, she could handle it, because living without him was not a choice. She loved him.

She loved Sean Knight.

Bo's gaze roamed over her face, and to her surprise, he smiled. "I'm not walking away from my work with you, Elise. But I am handing over your heart to Knight."

A noise broke from her, and she threw her arms around his neck. Clinging to him, a tear slithered down her cheek and was absorbed by his shirt. He gripped her against him in a platonic embrace — there had never been anything else between them — and understanding and peace settled over them both.

She stepped back, a new freedom and hope lifting her spirits. She felt like she could crack all the codes he put in front of her in one night if it meant seeing Sean soon.

She searched Bo's eyes. "He has to know I love him. I need to tell him. Take me to him."

Bo waved at the computer. "First, you've got to save yourself. How fast can you get your life back, Elise?"

"When you put it that way…" She hurried to the chair and sank into it, her fingers already tapping the keys.

* * * * *

Sean burst into Colonel Jackson's personal residence, his lungs burning with the need to bellow. He'd been in the big old Southern mansion once before, when Knight Ops had been invited to a barbecue for the colonel's birthday. Then he'd been asked by Ben to more or less kidnap the colonel's daughter, who Ben happened to be fucking. Still was. In fact, Sean and his family had been waiting for months for news of their wedding plans.

Hearing the door slam off the inner wall, Jackson strode into the grand foyer, weapon at the ready.

"Hell, it's you, Knight." He lowered his weapon. "Since when is it okay to storm a commanding officer's personal residence?"

Sean faced him. "Since when do you leave your door unlocked? I need to know where Elise Dupré is."

Jackson blinked. "Son, you know I can't give out that information. It's classified."

"I need to know, sir."

He eyed Sean. Damn if he didn't feel like a little kid being reprimanded by his father, made to stand and bear the man's scrutiny, knowing he saw far too much.

Sean's fingers convulsed into fists, but he stood his ground.

Jackson set his weapon aside on a table beside some mail and waved at Sean to follow him. With no other choice, Sean did. Over his shoulder, Jackson said, "Should I expect your brothers?"

"No, sir. They don't know I'm here." Sean's boots seemed to ring on the expensive tile floor. They went into Jackson's office, and he waved to a chair.

Sean took it, his back rigid. He only needed one piece of information and then this interview was over. He had to get out of here and find Elise—now. Not knowing where she was or if she was safe these past few days had worn him down until he felt a ticking like a bomb inside his chest.

Across his desk, Jackson looked at him. "What you did with *Rou* was nothing short of genius, Knight."

He grunted. He gave zero shits about what he'd just accomplished. Okay, maybe not zero but it was way down there on the list of his current priorities. First, he wanted to find Elise and kiss the hell out of her, right after telling her how he felt.

Saying he loved her was a huge achievement in its own right. Since walking away from her, his feelings had not only revealed themselves to him but smacked him between the eyes.

He needed her in his life—wasn't letting go.

"Sir, I just need to know about Elise."

"Hm. We'll get to that, Knight. Now what kind of colonel would I be if I didn't give praise where praise is due?"

Jesus, the man was settling into his leather seat to give Sean a rundown of his own actions. He had no choice but to grip the arms of his chair and listen.

"I've said this before, but your tactical skills are very sharp. I knew very early on in your time with Knight Ops that you're cut out for leadership. What you walked into in those swamps was an all-out war, and you handled yourself and your men with the highest honors."

"Thank you, sir." Why didn't Sean feel the pride he should in this situation? He'd always wanted to hear these things, and now here he sat, wishing he could speed Jackson along to get to the information he craved like water to a parched man.

"You saved your team's asses — and I don't just mean Rou. You kept Knight Ops from taking heavy fire too."

Sean's knee jerked up and down in a nervous action. He just needed to get to Elise. "I appreciate it, sir."

Jackson sat back in his seat, eagle eyes penetrating him. "You don't give a shit about a goddamn thing I'm saying, do you, Knight?"

"Uh, yes, sir. I give a shit about every goddamn thing you're saying."

Jackson flashed a smile. The man was a hard ass but eventually he'd be the father-in-law of Sean's brother, and maybe that earned them all special treatment. But Sean didn't hear him giving accolades to any other operators.

He waited, forcing his knee to still.

"There's a permanent position as leader open on Rou, and I'm offering it to you."

There it was. What he'd been waiting to hear for so many years.

Sean shoved out a breath and dragged in a new one. What he wanted dangled within reach, his for the taking. All he had to do was utter a simple *yes*.

Yet he sat there gaping at the colonel as if he didn't comprehend English.

A dozen things ran through his head. How would he break it to his brothers that he was walking away from them, no longer one of the Knight Ops unit? One of the reasons they were all so in sync was that they were related— watching each other's backs was a survival instinct, a primal need to protect and preserve family in all ways. Even Rocko had become like a sixth brother in the past few months, which meant Sean was capable of feeling the same about the guys of Team Rou.

And then there was Elise.

It galled him to have let her go into Hawkeye's hands. Though the man was capable, Sean did not like it one bit. He should be there for the woman he loved.

"I'll give you some time to consider my offer, Knight." Jackson broke into his thoughts.

He barely got out a nod.

"And I'll tell you about that woman you're so keen on finding."

He moved to the edge of his seat and his knee took up its violent jiggling again. "What about her, sir?"

Jackson's eyes narrowed as he obviously honed in on the internal battle Sean was waging. "I know you worked closely with her on decoding those messages, and that is also to be commended."

"All respect, Colonel, but I don't need praise. I'd just like to know where she is."

"I'll get to that. 'Elise,' as you call her, has managed to decipher more intel concerning her own safety."

His throat constricted, and he could hardly push air past it.

"And she has handled her own business."

Sean stared at Jackson. "What does that mean, sir?"

"Hawkeye might have acted as a handler, but she's never failed to take care of herself, and this time was no different."

"Sir?"

"She saved herself, Knight. 'Elise' is a very dangerous woman."

Relief swept him, and he felt his muscles relax. Sean's grin was unstoppable. His cheeks ached from the sudden movement of muscles that had been held so tensely in the past few days. "I know that, Colonel."

Jackson tipped his head back and released a laugh, leaving Sean in a state of shock. He'd never heard the colonel laugh in his life and had no idea he was even capable of making the sound.

If only the colonel knew just how dangerous that woman was to Sean's heart... Still grinning, he shook his head.

Jackson stood, as intimidating in his khaki pants and polo shirt as he was in full uniform. Sean snapped to his feet, at attention.

"Thanks to your quick thinking that has the warheads secured and the Russians under lock and key and being interrogated as we speak, the threat has passed. And your lady friend was able to return home. She should be on her way there right now."

Sean took two steps toward the door before he realized he needed to take leave of the colonel first. He strode back to salute him, but Jackson held out a hand for him to shake. Sean took it and pumped it hard, once.

"Thank you, sir."

"Think about Rou, Knight."

As he rushed back out to his El Camino and gunned it down the long drive flanked by Magnolia trees, he couldn't think of anything but Elise. How she'd feel in his arms as he plunged his tongue between her lips and tasted her. Then wiggling under him as he tongued her hot pussy.

He had no idea how she'd react to him confessing his love, but he was more than ready to find her and do just that, his mind far from Jackson, Team Rou or Knight Ops.

Chapter Ten

"Well Tyleri finally did it." Chaz's tone was as ominous as a massive coronary as he referred to their little sister by nickname. Sean, Ben and the rest of them snapped their gazes to him. He clutched his cell in one hand, a vein pulsing in his neck that could only mean the worst had happened.

"Jesus, just tell us. What did Tyler do?" Ben shot out, looking about to go off the deep end.

Sean held his breath, and he felt his other brothers moving in to create a semi-circle around Chaz.

Chaz looked up, his face a mask. "She's run away and joined the Marines."

Silence shrouded them, and for a long minute, nobody spoke.

"Run away?" Ben echoed.

"Joined the Marines?" Sean asked. "Jesus Christ."

Roades shook his head, backing up a step. Sean pierced him in his gaze. "You knew about this," Sean said.

He shook his head.

"You're closer to her in age. Did she confide in you she was doing this?" Ben demanded, more captain than brother at this moment.

Roades held up both palms. Sean looked closely at his youngest brother, wondering when the hell he'd grown into his cocky attitude. At the age of twenty-one, he seemed to have shot up two inches since Sean last looked at him. And was it even possible that his shoulders were as wide as his own? Roades was a damn puppy, so hell no, it wasn't possible.

"I didn't know anything about Tyler's plans and if I had, she wouldn't have gone. I would have used Sean's zip-ties and she'd be in her bedroom at home right now."

Dylan shoved his fingers through his hair. "Why the hell would she do such a thing? Knowing what we face daily?"

Sean raised his brows at Dylan. They'd always known Tyler was impulsive to the extreme, and she'd been a tomboy pretty much since sliding out of the womb. It didn't help that she'd been saddled with a male name. None of this should shock any of them, and Sean opened his mouth to say so when Ben spoke up.

"There's nothing to do now. She'll have to work hard to follow our footsteps. And I hate to say it, but being a woman will be even tougher to overcome."

Staring at his phone, Chaz's face turned red and then purple.

Sean and Ben charged him at the same time, Sean pinning his arm behind his back while Ben snatched the phone from him. He stared at the screen and then his own face turned a bright hue.

"What the hell is it?" Sean demanded.

Ben held out the cell and they all gaped at a selfie of their little sister dressed as a male, her wavy hair clippered to a buzz cut and her breasts hidden under a loose T-shirt.

"Jesus, she's trying to enlist as a male? Even without her usual makeup, she's still obviously a woman. How far does she think she'll go in that getup?" Sean asked, releasing Chaz.

Ben scowled. "Sooner or later she'll have a physical and she won't pass the cough test."

They all chuckled.

"Damn crazy girl. Can you believe she shaved her head?" Ben asked.

"I can." Sean peered at the photo again. "She knew damn well she wouldn't get through as a male, but she had to try to pull one over. It's total Tyler style."

"Shit." The quiet expression came from Dylan.

They all turned to him.

"That leaves Lexi unchaperoned, alone at home, and we all know she'll outsmart *Maman* and *Pére* and land herself in big trouble without Tyler keeping an eye on her."

They groaned. "You mean bigger trouble than usual. That just means we need to stick close to home as often as possible. Go in shifts if necessary," Ben said.

"Why don't you and Dahlia take the first shift? Good luck keeping your moans down so our parents don't hear you." Sean's wry tone had them all laughing, but he was more than ready to end this family reunion and get to his own moaning.

Ben smirked. "Fine. I'll take first shift. But you assholes better be ready to back me up."

"Sean's next, and he's bringing Elise," Dylan said.

They all looked to him. Sean nodded. "Just as soon as we get some alone time to moan. I'll see you punks later."

He started away from the group and toward the lot where his El Camino was parked.

"Hey, wait up," Ben called.

He turned to see his brother jogging toward him. Sean stopped walking and waited. Ben stopped before him.

"I heard what Jackson offered you. I just wanted you to know that I talked to the guys and we all give you our blessings."

His chest grew hot and tight at the thought of walking away from his brothers, his team. He shook his head. "I still haven't given Jackson an answer."

"You'll say yes. It's what you've been wanting. It's what you deserve." Respect shone in Ben's eyes, and that tight feeling swelled up into Sean's throat.

He couldn't speak, only gave another nod.

Ben clapped him on the shoulder. "Get goin'. Women will only wait so long."

"Take your own advice," Sean shot back and hurried to his vehicle. His mind raced with what had happened back in that swamp, and with having his own team after all these years in active duty.

But right now, he had other important things to think about.

Like getting the old El Camino up to top speed so he could reach Elise sooner.

* * * * *

214

"Oh my God! Sean." Elise yanked him through the door into her apartment and threw herself at him. He made an *oomph* sound but brought his arms around her, dragging her into the tightest hug she'd ever had.

He pushed the door closed and bowed his head against hers, drawing deep breaths. She did the same, so happy to have his scent filling her head once more.

"That was the longest thirty-six hours I've ever lived through." Her words were muffled against his chest.

"I know, *cher.*" He sounded choked, and she drew back to look up into his eyes. They were troubled, the depths as dark as a storm on the horizon.

But she didn't get a chance to ask, because he slammed his mouth over hers. The kiss bruising, demanding. His beard stubble scraped her sensitive skin as he probed her lips with his tongue, forcing entry.

She gave in to him with a gasp, need compounding. As he swept the interior of her mouth with his tongue once... twice... a slow burn exploded into a fiery need.

He felt it too, judging by the bulge in his jeans. Gripping her hips, he walked her back against the door, pinning her with his steely body and heady passes of his tongue. Passion didn't just trickle through her — it gushed. She

215

lifted her leg and wrapped her thigh around his hips.

When he dug his erection into her throbbing pussy, they shared a groan.

"I can't wait to get you to a bed," he growled each word.

"Who wants a bed?" She tore at his shirt, exposing all those swells and cuts. She pattered her fingers over his torso, feeling for new wounds, but found none. Relief hit, but he wiped that emotion off her mind when he whipped up her shirt, ducked his head and sucked her nipple through her bra.

Her eyes fluttered shut on a wave of pleasure. She dug her blunt nails into his shoulders, clinging as he wet through her bra and tendrils of heat struck her skin. Need burst inside her, and she couldn't hold back anymore.

She went for his waistband, eagerness making her fingers clumsy, but she managed to open his jeans and slip her hand into his briefs.

"Ffffuck." He scraped his teeth up the curve of her breast as she curled her fingers around his shaft. Steel wrapped in velvet, the head swollen and the tip slick with his arousal.

He plucked the clasp of her bra and it snapped open. She shimmied to let it drop to the floor and leaned in to swirl her tongue over the eagle wings stretching over his pec even as she pumped his cock through her fist.

"I can't fool around with foreplay, *cher*. I need you—now." The darkness lingering in his eyes was a complete and utter turn-on, practically scorching the rest of her clothes off her.

He dropped his jeans to his ankles and fisted a condom into place while kissing her into delirium. She drank in his taste and let her heart have full rein. Each moment she had with this man was a gift, a lesson she'd learned over the past couple days. She wasn't going to take any of it for granted.

He lifted her thigh high on his hip, bent his knees and filled her with one surge. She cried out as he stretched her wet inner walls, burying the flared head of his cock against her deepest point.

At that second, the words she'd begged Bo to take her to Sean so she could tell him spilled out.

"I love you, Sean. I love you so damn much."

He went dead still, not moving or breathing. Her pussy clenched around him once, bringing him back to life.

He stared down into her eyes, his jaw set and a muscle fluttering in the crease. "You love me?" His gritty tone was nothing but tender. Her heart flipped and broke open wider to accept him into it.

She nodded.

"Jesus, I don't deserve you." He plunged his cock into her again, and she was so excited by her admission and the heat of the moment, it was all she needed to start contracting around him in a haze of bliss.

He fucked her harder, pulling her screams from her and feeding moan after moan back to her. The assault on her pussy with his hard cock sent her higher and higher until a second orgasm struck.

"I'm coming, baby. Filling up your sweet pussy." He threw his head back, neck tendons straining as his own release hit. The liquid warmth he spilled wasn't enough for her — she wanted him with no barriers and would tell him in the next ten steps it took to reach her bedroom.

She barely came off her high with a shiver, and he lowered his mouth to her neck, her ear, sliding up and down between them. "You love me?" he asked again.

She squeezed his ass, causing him to rock into her deeper. She moaned and turned her lips against his forehead. "I do. Sean, I was going crazy that I couldn't tell you. Knowing you were out in the field, your life on the line..." She swallowed against the sudden lump in her throat.

A shudder coursed through him, and he pressed a soft kiss to her jaw and then the corner of her mouth. He pulled back to look into her eyes. "I thought I'd lose my mind, Elise. Sending you off, not knowing if you'd be safe..." He choked off the words. "I guess it was a moment of reckoning for both of us."

She searched his eyes. "What do you mean?"

"I love you too, *cher*." He lifted his gaze to her hair and zigzagged it over her features until he zeroed in on her mouth. "Everything about you from your tough exterior to your brilliant mind. God, Elise, I can't believe you feel the same about me." He closed his eyes and tipped his forehead against hers.

Love bloomed in her all over again, and she kissed his lean cheeks and nibbled at his lips.

"Take me to bed, special operator Knight," she whispered.

She felt his smile. "Mmm. I'll show you my skills."

"You'd better after that short fuck against the door you just gave me." She swatted his ass, delivering a loud crack that echoed in the space.

His chest rumbled with laughter. "Are you testin' me already, woman? I thought we'd at least get past the honeymoon before you started with that."

Honeymoon? Damn, this was going fast, and she couldn't help but warm inside at the thought of what would come between them. He was in love with her too, and for now that was overwhelming enough.

She hooked her arms around his neck and used her core strength to shimmy up him, locking her heels around his broad back.

"Baby, the condom's slipping. I—"

"Shhh," she said against his lips. "I've got an implant. And the next round, I want your hot come shooting inside me."

"Fucking hell," he said as if on a prayer.

"Uh-huh. Now get me to the bedroom, Sean. I'm not waiting more than a minute for you to put your mouth on my pussy."

"Oh God. You're definitely going to kill me." His grin gave her a wolfish flash of white teeth that only had her aching all over again.

* * * * *

Elise's honey brown skin glowed in the waning light of the day. Sean gazed at her.

Sleeping on her side, arm curled beneath her head and dark hair spread over her shoulders, she could be a goddess.

She loved him.

He'd found someone who gave a shit if he lived or died out there, but now that he had that person, terror filled him.

What if something did happen to him? He'd leave her broken. The thought only fed into his tension until he slipped from the bed and pulled on his jeans. Pacing would wake her—his *maman* always said he sounded like a herd of cattle walking through the house—so he sank to an upholstered bench on the side of the room. Frilly pillows spilled onto his lap and he squeezed one over and over as he stared at the woman in his life.

How did Ben do it? Give himself to Dahlia without these worries stealing all joy from their love? He had no idea how to deal with this shit—he was a Marine. Able to snap the neck of an enemy without pause if the situation called for it. Yet his hands had just roamed all over Elise's body, loving her in ways he'd never imagined himself capable of.

When he looked down at the pillow in his hands, he found it crumpled and misshapen. He tried to fluff it, but the sound of him smacking it around woke Elise.

She sat up and cracked an eye at him. "What are you doing to my pillow?"

"Uh." He set it aside. "Sorry. I'll buy you a new one."

Concern drew her brows downward. "What's the matter? If you're thinking of running out on me now, I'm here to tell you — "

He crossed to the bed in two steps and gathered her into his arms. "Not that. Never that. I guess I'm just letting my mind run away with me is all."

She eyed him. "Meaning?"

He smoothed her hair back from her temple and pressed a light kiss between her brows. They unfurrowed but she still looked about to sock him in the nuts if he said something she didn't like. He almost chuckled — the problems of loving a warrior woman. She wasn't going to take any crap, and he liked that.

"Sean." Her voice held a warning.

"I was just thinking how dangerous my position is. If something happened, I don't like to think about how you'd feel."

"Don't even talk about it then. Marine code, right? We run in and do our jobs without thinking of anything but doing it well."

He studied her beautiful face. "You're right."

"Besides, I could leave you in the same position."

His heart sank. He knew it, but hearing it was another thing.

He drew her more fully against him. "There's something I need to talk to you about, Elise."

She pushed back. "I don't like the sound of that."

He shoved his fingers through his hair and wracked his brain for words. He'd spent a long time thinking about how to tell her about Team Rou and the leadership position, but he had nothing rehearsed. He was winging it.

Like so many other things in his life.

"Sean, just say it." She spread her hands.

He gave a short nod. "Jackson offered me Team Rou."

She stared at him blankly for a long heartbeat. Then she dropped her gaze to her fingers that were tangled in her lap. "Captain?"

"Yes."

"I figured something like this was coming. Bo mentioned..."

"You talked to Bo about this?"

"He just told me how well you'd done in leading Rou on that operation."

"Ah." As much as he wanted to dislike Hawkeye's permanent fixture status in her life, he couldn't. The man had kept her safe, and Sean was grateful. Besides, now that Hawk knew he wasn't a threat to their relationship, he didn't mind him being around Elise, ex-husband or not.

"Sean, I think you should take the position."

He looked up at her, surprised. "But you know what it means. I'd be more of a target. I'd put myself in more danger to keep the rest of the team safe."

"I know," she said softly. "It's what we do. But do you want this?"

His chest swelled as he drew in a deep breath. Hell yeah, he'd wanted this for so long. Being second in command got old, especially when it was your big brother's ass you were kissin'.

He nodded. "Dammit, I do want it."

"Then take it." Her words were short as she swung her legs off the bed and stood.

Uh-oh. He didn't' like that reaction. At all.

He moved to take her hands. She stood in all her glory of nudeness before him, and he wanted to dip his head and suck her dark nipple into his mouth until he felt it bud on his tongue. But he resisted. They needed to sort this out—it was their first foray into a relationship issue, and he wanted to start things off right. With her input.

"Elise, is that what you really think I should do? What about what you want?"

A soft smile tilted her lips as she shook her head. "Sean, if it were me, I'd jump at the opportunity. You should too. Each of us knows what the other faces as far as danger goes. We wouldn't be the people we are if we didn't do these things. Hell, would we even like each other if I was say, a teacher, and you a construction worker?"

"What if I was the teacher and you a construction worker?" He caught her eyes and smiled.

She laughed. "That's just as likely. But you know what I mean. Sean, take the promotion. You've earned it. You deserve it."

His eyes closed on her words as his heart expanded with more love for this woman. He had a feeling in their years to come, that organ would grow a hell of a lot just to fit all these things to love about her into it.

He wrapped his arms around her waist and pulled her against him. His lips were on a level just beneath her breasts, and he tipped his head up to lap at the soft undercurve of one.

She sucked in a breath, and it was game on. He started kissing across one to the other, moving back and forth and then tracing the small ridges of her flat stomach down to the triangle of hair covering the sweet treasure he wanted — needed — to taste.

She gasped and sank her fingers into his hair. "Yes, Sean. God, yes."

Chapter Eleven

Sean threw Elise a look. "You nervous?" He gripped the pole he used to dig into the bottom of the swamp and propel the small boat to his family cabin.

She shook her head, and her ponytail bobbed. "I know Marines and their families. Remember?"

He was afraid of that. Hell, he found his family annoying and intimidating at times—how could she not?

Using his upper body strength, he pushed off the soft bottom again. The raft floated ten more feet. "Not much farther."

"I hear the music," she said.

When they got together at the cabin, his family really let go and had an all-out Cajun party with music, alcohol and more food than any person should consume in one day. It had been a while since they'd all gathered here, and Sean was actually looking forward to it.

"I'll get to meet your sisters too?" Elise asked.

He pushed off. Sweat zigzagged down his neck. "One of them. My younger sister Tyler took off and joined the Marines the other day."

She gaped up at him. "You didn't tell me."

He grinned. "We haven't done much talkin', *cher*."

She got that deeper color in her cheeks that told him she was blushing. "Was this unknown to all of you, I take it?"

He nodded. "She's been threatenin' to join up since she was twelve, but none of us believed her. I never would have guessed she'd shave her head and try to go in as a male either."

"What?" Elise's jaw dropped.

"She won't have gotten far, but for Tyler, it's all about trying to pull one over on you."

"Girl's got guts." Elise's tone sounded with admiration.

"Should I be worried that you seem to identify with my sister?"

She crossed her legs. In cutoff shorts, they'd been tormenting him since he'd watched her dress that morning. "Worried? No. You already know what I'm capable of, Sean Knight. So don't try to pull anything over on *me*. And you can stop looking at my legs now. I just got a bit of drool on my thigh."

He made an exaggerated move with his tongue to wet his lips that had her squirming on the wooden seat. "You know what I want to do with those shorts when we get home."

"I know…" She seemed to be playing the footage of it in her head right now, if the way her nipples bunched under her top was any indication.

They passed a clump of trees, dodging low-hanging branches, and then the cabin came into sight. Each time Sean saw it, his heart warmed with happy feelings. He wanted Elise to feel the same in coming here. Someday he wanted them to bring their children and show them the fun of gator hunting, fishing and general family fun unplugged from the world.

Unplugged was a loose term, however. There might not be electricity or cell service, but last time Ben's satellite phone had rung and they'd all rushed out on an operation.

Now Sean carried a satellite phone too.

He'd been in touch with all the guys from his team just to tell them how proud he was to be leading them, and he'd gotten verbal pats on the back from each. The good feelings only went so far, though, when he was guilt-ridden for running out on Knight Ops.

He hadn't seen his brothers face-to-face since accepting the promotion, and part of him feared he'd be met with attitude. But Ben would have paved the way with the others, so he hoped he wasn't facing any arguments or masked hostilities today.

He wanted this experience to be the most pleasant for Elise.

When they reached the dock, Elise leaned over the side to grab it without being told.

"You've done this before."

"Uh...With Bo."

"Ah."

There were still some hurdles there for Sean to leap, but he was trying, dammit. So what if he wanted to get the guy on the ground and smack him around a little bit? That was just guy stuff, right?

Elise grabbed the rope and tied them off on a post. "Look," she said without looking at him, "it's in my past. I can't apologize for living before I met you." She met his stare, and he nodded.

"You're right." He stepped onto the dock and reached down for her hand. She placed it in his and he drew her out of the boat. The music was loud, and nobody was outside the cabin, which was odd considering the weatherman had given the clearest blue sky for their gathering. But Sean took the moment to be alone with Elise.

He cupped her face. "I'm sorry if I seem like an ass when it comes to your ex. I'm trying."

She smiled softly. "I know. I'd be irritated too if you were best friends with your ex and she came into your closet and picked out your clothes for you."

"Wait. What?"

Just them Lexi spilled out of the cabin and squealed when she saw them. Sean released Elise and turned to greet his baby sister, but from the corner of his mouth, he said to Elise, "You're going to explain that later."

"No doubt." Amusement tinged her words as she slapped a smile on her face for Lexi.

"Oh my God, Sean. You look so grown-up now. Like a *captain*." Lexi walked up to him and threw her arms around his neck.

He hugged her back, lifting her off her feet and swinging her off the dock so her whole body dangled over the swamp, something they'd done since she was a little girl.

She shrieked right in his ear hole, deafening him, and he laughed as he swung her back to put her bare feet on the wooden dock. He stuffed his forefinger into his ear and wiggled it.

"Damn, girl. You can still scream the same."

"Someone must be dangling Lex over the dock again. Could only be Sean." Dylan's drawl reached him as he came outside too, followed by Chaz holding a beer.

Sean released his sister and slipped an arm around Elise's waist. "Lexi, Chaz, this is Elise. You know Dylan. These are my other two extreme siblings," he said to Elise.

She had smiles for all and shook hands.

"What do you mean by extreme?" Lexi said with narrowed eyes.

"Only that you two are the risk-takers of the family."

"Seriously? What about Tyler?" Lexi tapped a foot, the aqua toenails gleaming in the sun.

"We've already discussed Tyler," he said. "Elise, you want a beer?" He took her by the hand and led her into the cabin.

Immediately, *Maman* turned from stirring a huge pot that, from the smell of it, was her famous low boil. Sean's stomach growled.

His mother bustled across the room to them and hugged Sean and then Elise, to her surprise. She slanted an amused smile at him as his mother let her go. "I'm so happy to see you here, Sean. We didn't know with your new team and all…"

Sean gave his mother a smile and introduced Elise. They talked for a moment about what was for dinner before he led Elise across the room to where Roades and their father sat at the table, dismantling a generator. Greasy parts were scattered over an old towel, and both of them were absorbed in the workings.

Roades glanced up, a black smudge across his jaw. "Look what the gator dragged in."

"Nah, I got the gator in the boat ready for roastin'." Sean could see a hesitation on Roades' face that he didn't like. He was afraid of this—if one of his brothers wasn't on board with him leaving Knight Ops, it would be the youngest male among them. As kids, Roades had pal'd around with Sean the most, and their bond was strong.

"*Pére*, Roades, this is Elise."

She gave them a smile that charmed the scales off one of those gators they'd mentioned, and Roades actually returned it.

"Glad to have you in the family, Elise." *Pére* looked up with a gleam in his eyes.

"Thank you, sir."

"No sir around here. Well, unless you're talkin' to Ben or Sean. You can call me Chip."

Elise's smile widened. Their father had a way of drawing people in, and the Knights had always joked they'd gotten their hard-ass military tendencies from their mother.

Sean met his stare and gave a small nod. It was the only exchange he and his father would need when it came to acknowledging his new role as captain.

A bit of tension Sean hadn't known he carried eased from his shoulders, and he pressed a kiss to Elise's temple. "Want a beer?"

"Sure. All that poling through the swamp made me thirsty."

He laughed because he'd been doing all the work but didn't say so as he went out onto the deck to grab two beers from the cooler.

Chaz and Dylan were kicked back on the dock, rigging their fishing poles and shooting the shit. Sean paused near them for a moment.

Dylan looked up. "You finally got the girl."

"Looks that way." He grinned.

"Wasn't your brains that snagged her."

"Probably not, since she far exceeds me in brain power. Must have been all this." He ran a hand over his abs, and Chaz made puking noises.

Dylan smirked. "I'm happy for you. Really."

Sean looked at him closer. "Happy for my promotion too?"

"Of course," Dylan said at once. "You earned it, bro." He held out his fist, and Sean bumped his knuckles against it.

"Chaz? You good with the changes?"

"People come and go in units. And the new guy's good. Probably even a better shot than you."

Sean grunted. "Asshole. You just had to get that jab in." Chaz was forever touting his own weapons skills and challenging Sean whenever he could.

Sean cuffed him in the ear, and Chaz smacked him in the balls with the handle of his fishing rod. The blow caught the very edge of his left nut, and he folded in half to recover just as Elise came outside.

"Here's your beer," he squeaked in a high voice that had her giggling.

"Which one of you bested this guy?"

"Are you going to avenge me, *cher*?" Sean asked.

She laughed and accepted her beer. "No, I want to shake his hand." That had them all laughing.

"That'd be me." Chaz extended a hand for her to shake.

Sean recovered and straightened, happy with the exchange. Elise was used to dealing with rough guys, and she'd fit right in.

She leaned close and dropped a kiss to Sean's cheek. "You all right, hon?"

"I'm fine. Don't you worry about my baby-making abilities."

"Umm, we'll discuss that down the road." Her soft smile and the luminous expression in her eyes had his heart welling with love for her, though. "I'm going back inside and help your *maman*."

He felt like he'd burst with happiness. "I think I'll do some fishin' with these idiots. If you need me, I'll be here."

She nodded and went back inside. Sean took a seat on the dock and reached for one of the poles and some bait. With the sun beating down on them and the scents of good food wafting from the cabin, he couldn't feel happier. His family, besides Roades, was happy for him. And at least he'd left Knight Ops knowing their sixth member was a good shot.

Still, it niggled at him that he wouldn't know everything that went down with the team. Since the inception, each operation had brought them all closer. Would he be left on the edges of the group now that he wouldn't share those experiences with them?

He shook off the thought. This opportunity wasn't to be missed. He'd wanted it forever, and before Jackson had gathered them all into

Knight Ops, the brothers had been scattered far and wide and yet they'd still managed to come together.

A boat came through the trees, and a hoot of greeting sounded from Ben, with Dahlia seated next to him.

Sean made a sign to shed off the evil spirits. "Look at this swamp creature coming for us."

"Speak for yourself, Rougarou," Ben said as he caught the edge of the dock and tied off the boat. He wore a grin but there was a reservation in his eyes that Sean didn't like. Now he had two brothers to get alone and make peace with. Ben and Roades were too close in personality for all of their comfort.

Lexi bounced outside to drag Dahlia off, and their father and Roades drifted out to grab some poles too, the generator abandoned for a few hours.

Sean glanced toward the cabin.

"She's fine with the ladies," Ben said. He raised a beer to his lips. "Trust me."

Sean nodded. "It's weird, isn't it? This need to protect them at all times."

Ben's eyes gleamed but he said nothing. It was enough for Sean to know he understood and agreed—he just wasn't willing to voice it in front of the others, if at all.

They sat side by side sipping beer, their lines in the water. Sean needed to address what was on his mind, especially before dinner hit the table and after, when the guitars and banjos were pulled out.

"You good with what went down, man?" he asked Ben.

He looked up. "Of course. Told you I was, didn't I?"

"Just checkin'."

"We'll do fine without you. Gallagher is a great addition to Knight Ops, even though he's suggested we call it Gallagher Ops."

Sean chuckled and clasped his brother's shoulder. "Promise me you won't let that happen."

"At this point, I think the order would have to come down from above. But we all wish you the best."

Sean looked to Roades seated on the other side of their father, staring across the swamp.

Ben followed his line of sight. "Yeah, he's taken it harder than the rest of us. You always were his hero, Sean."

That brought a tightness to Sean's throat that he couldn't speak around even if he had words. After a minute and a couple sips of beer, he said, "I don't even know how to smooth things over there."

"He'll come around in time. He wants the best for you, but a team is always like family. Except ours *is* family. Makes it rougher."

Sean nodded. Ben was stoic about it, but having been in the Marines the longest, he'd come to accept anything over the years. Just about the only thing that would rile him now was some threat to Dahlia.

The ladies drifted outside and took seats around the big picnic table. That was the men's cue to get up and carry out the food, a tradition among the Knight family. When Sean got up, he caught Elise's gaze on him, and damn if her plump lips weren't parted in that I-so-want-you way he was all too familiar with after only a few days with her.

With his cock stirring at the mere look on her face, he ducked under the doorframe and grabbed one of the big platters full of shellfish and corn with spices.

One by one the guys placed the food on the table before the women who'd helped prepare it. Sean couldn't help but think that one day, each of his brothers would have a woman they loved seated here looking at them the same way Elise was looking at him.

He sank to the bench next to her and leaned close to whisper in her ear. "I saw the way you were looking at me, *cher*. Don't think I'll let that slip by."

* * * * *

Elise put on her running shoes and went out the door, locking it behind her. The air was cool this morning and hopefully that and the exercise would help her clear her head. She needed a long run to escape the claustrophobic feeling of being in her apartment and knowing Sean was out there leading Team Rou on a dangerous mission.

Worse, that he couldn't even tell her about it.

She did some cursory stretching exercises and then took off at a light jog. Within minutes, though, she hit her pace. Running through New Orleans in the morning was one of her favorite things. She loved this city, and now that she had Sean to share it with her, she loved it more.

The previous evening he'd taken her to one of the best restaurants and somehow gotten past the waiting list and straight to a table, where they'd gotten the best service. When she asked him who he knew to get that preferential treatment, he'd only given that private smile and shook his head.

Then, mere hours later he'd again given her the close-lipped side of himself when he'd told her he was headed out and would be back as soon as he could.

She pushed out a breath and dragged in another, driving herself to run faster. Exhaustion might be the only thing that shut her brain up for a while.

But if she wanted to continue in a relationship with a man in OFFSUS, she had to get used to this... this not knowing. This fear.

She ran past huge old painted ladies, the houses standing sentry in the early dawn, their colors seeming to glow from some inner spirit of the homes. She adored this district, but it was the coast that called to her, the sand where she and Sean had run for miles. She stretched her stride and focused on running. Before she knew it, she was standing in front of the inn where she and Sean had stayed while decoding those messages. The place where they'd first gotten physical and if she was honest with herself, the place where she'd fallen in love with him. Of course, she hadn't admitted it to herself then, but now she saw it clearly.

An idea hit, and she went inside the inn, hoping her sweaty appearance didn't put off the innkeeper. She rang a bell at the front desk, and a woman came from the back, a smile on her face.

"Hi, can I help you?" She glanced over Elise's appearance of running attire.

"Sorry about the early hour. I was out for a run and had an idea. I'd like to book a room for a couple days."

"Sure. When would you like to come?" She went to her book and opened it to a calendar.

"Um... I'm not sure." When would Sean be home? It could be days, weeks, months? Oh God, she couldn't think about that. She hoped OFFSUS would keep them close to home in the South, but she knew the Knight Ops team had been sent overseas not long ago, and that was where they'd gained their overnight notoriety.

She swallowed. "I guess I need to plan better." She gave a short, nervous laugh, and the woman responded with a reflexive smile. "I'll make a call when I know the dates."

"That sounds perfect. I look forward to hearing from you."

Elise went out of the inn and hit the sand again, her feet pounding this time until her shins ached. She slowed, taking care to put her feet down softer.

As she circled back in the direction of her apartment, she thought of Bo. Whenever she was upset, she'd always call him and even if he couldn't fix her problem, he was there for her. A solid presence that was comforting. But somehow, consoling herself with her ex's attention when she was pining over another man felt off.

She had to get through this on her own.

She'd just have to stay busy. After her run, she'd have a long soak in the tub and walk down to the market and shop for something good for dinner. Maybe stock up on some strawberries and fresh cream in hopes her man returned sooner than expected and she could use him as a man buffet to eat those treats off his hard body.

A low quiver in her belly told her she'd better take it one step at a time. When he came home, however, she wasn't wasting a moment before getting what she wanted.

Chapter Twelve

The strong scent of roasting meat reached Sean, and he pressed the button on his comms unit. "Do you fuckers need to eat that swamp rat right now?"

Earlier, two of his men had caught several nutrias and promised a barbecue for dinner. Out here in the middle of nowhere, people ate anything they could, but right now, Sean was focused on staying undetected until their target came in—a man rumored to be dealing in the slave trade. A disgusting motherfucker with a record that would curl the hairs of even the most hardened criminal. The man wasn't just rumored to partake in cannibalism of the people he enslaved—it was documented.

The scent of roasting meat turned Sean's stomach.

"Good stuff, Cap'n. There's plenty. Come'n get it," Wolf drawled.

"I'm good," he said tightly, breathing shallowly to keep the smell from hitting the back of his throat and making him gag. He and his brothers had eaten a few of the rats in his lifetime, but they were kids and by the time he'd hit ten years old, he'd developed better taste buds.

Noises came from Wolf. Sean shook his head, a laugh on his lips. "Are you fucking licking your lips, Wolf? You sick bastard."

"Next we'll cook up some frog legs for ya, Cap'n."

"As long as you got butter to dip them in, I'm on board." Actually, his stomach rumbled. He had a couple MREs—or meals ready to eat—on him, but he wasn't eager to tear into the chicken parmesan that was made to withstand a fucking apocalypse just yet.

He thought of his last meal with Elise. Her skin glowing in the candlelight, as romantic as he'd ever gotten with a woman. Watching her savor each bite of her scallops had made him as hard as a fucking rock, and he'd barely gotten her out of the El Camino before he was feeling her up. Hand under her skirt, plucking at the tiny strip of fabric covering her pussy as he kissed her and walked her up the steps to her door.

His cock shifted under his fly now, and he cut off that train of thought. He had far too many hours to go before he saw her again. Getting a supreme case of blue balls wasn't in the spec ops playbook today.

Quiet banter came back to him from the men, and he smiled at their antics that ranged from chest-thumping, one-upping each other to all-out ribbing Frisco about nailing some waitress the night before.

That was when Sean learned how Frisco got his nickname—apparently his last three girlfriends had come from San Francisco.

They weren't any different from any team he'd ever fought with—not even Knight Ops. He wondered what they were talking about right now. Hunkered down somewhere too, listening to Chaz talk about who he'd taken to his bed and then given cab fare to instead of a text in the morning.

He shook his head. He missed his brothers, even if he'd just seen them at the cabin. And he ached for Elise in a way he'd never thought possible before falling in love with her.

All the crickets in the swamp seemed to have congregated around him and were singing so loudly that he had to crank the volume of his earpiece. Just in time to hear a grunt.

A grunt of pain.

All the hair stood up on his forearms and he raised his weapon. "McMahon, is that you?"

"Jesus, he's hit. He's hit, guys. McMahon's down."

Adrenaline struck Sean, and he moved from his crouch to a stand, thighs protesting the cramped position he'd held for far too long. He forced his muscles to move and hit the ground running. Swamp water splashed up his legs and flowed over his boots into his socks, but he had to get there.

"I got ya, man. Hold on." That came from Corporon, and Sean did not like the strain in his tone one fucking bit. It told him more about McMahon's condition than anything but seeing the man for himself could.

His heart pumped faster, and he rounded a group of cypress where his men were positioned.

Another shot fired past Sean's head, and he dodged sideways. Motherfucker was shooting at him, and the asshole'd made the grave error of shooting a man on his team.

Now *he* was going to the grave.

Leaving the care of McMahon to the others, Sean stormed into the grove of trees, all stealth gone. This was what happened when you were captain—you put your life on the line to protect the rest of your team, and he went without thought.

Another shot zipped past him, and he didn't realize he'd been hit until he smelled the burning of fabric. He glanced down at his shoulder to see a furrow ripped through his sleeve and blood pooling in the opening.

Rage hit him, and he felt those hard pounding rhythms of his heart that secretly he considered to be the reason for his nickname. Thunder.

Well, he was about to open up the heavens on this goddamn threat.

"Thunder, wait for backup."

He ignored it, didn't stop. Because other words were filling his ear. "McMahon, hold on. Goddammit, look at me. Don't close your eyes. Jesus, he's bleeding out too fast. Someone give me something to make a tourniquet."

"You can't tourniquet a neck, Corporon. McMahon, buddy, you're all right. Just stay calm. We're getting you out."

But something told Sean that he was about to get a crash course in team leadership—by losing his first man.

Pain mixed with fury as he pinned his target in the scope of his weapon and took the shot. If anybody was going down today, it was the man who deserved it.

* * * * *

Sean's collar was too tight, choking him. He hadn't been in full dress blues for a long time. How soon he'd adjusted to T-shirts and cargo pants.

His sweaty palm slipped on the handle of the coffin and he held on tighter. He wasn't about to fail his buddy McMahon by letting him fall a second time. It was bad enough he'd let him down once.

Ahead of Sean, Frisco's shoulders were stiff. And on the other side of the casket were more of his men, fighting to hide their grief that one of them had been killed.

Sean kept his gaze straight ahead and walked, putting aside his own feelings. Truth be told, he was fucking gutted. Sure, he'd heard it all from Jackson and his brothers—men put their lives on the line for their country every day, and McMahon had gone out in a blaze of honor.

Guts and glory, he thought of the Knight Ops motto. But this wasn't Knight Ops and McMahon shouldn't have lost his life.

The scents of grass filled his nose with each step he took through the cemetery toward the group of mourners gathered there.

When they stopped and lowered the coffin to rest on a pedestal next to the open grave, a loud sob drew Sean's head up. He met the eyes of McMahon's mother.

Fuck, all that pain. A huge waste of life. For what? Because some idiot wanted to remain hidden and continue torturing people.

But then Sean looked around and found Elise, standing there with her fingers clasped and looking so striking in a black dress that skimmed her curves in such elegance that it made him swallow hard.

Their gazes connected.

It could have been me.

But it wasn't, hers seemed to say.

It might be next time.

Can you really give up because you're scared?

He wasn't scared—not for himself. But he never, ever wanted Elise to be the one standing there sobbing for him. Or his own *maman.*

The service was a blur, and then he and the rest of Team Rou paid their respects, giving their team handshake and then thumping the side of the coffin before walking away.

Elise clutched Sean's hand, and he realized someone else was flanking her other side. Hawkeye.

Sean nodded to the man.

"Fucking hard loss," Hawk said.

"Yeah."

"I knew McMahon a long time. We were friends back in high school. Ran these swamps like ghosts. I can't believe it was him when I heard."

Sean tightened his lips. He knew pain, but it was nothing like what Hawk must be experiencing for his long-time buddy.

"Well, I'm going home to visit my *maman* this afternoon," Hawk said.

"Give her my best." Elise put her hand on his arm.

He nodded and walked off, leaving them alone.

All the way back to Elise's apartment, Sean was silent, and she left him to his own thoughts. But as soon as they entered the house, she pulled him down on the couch and then curled up in his lap.

He put his arms around her and buried his nose in her hair, drawing deep breaths of her sweetness.

"You couldn't have done anything more, you know," she said softly.

"I know." He pushed out a sigh. "I'll be okay."

She nodded against him. "I know you will. But can I do anything for you right now? You want a sandwich or something?"

The last thing he wanted was food, but he realized he hadn't eaten in a long time and she needed to keep herself busy, to feel like she was doing something for him. He nodded. "Ham would be great."

She gave him a small smile and climbed off his lap. She took a moment to shed her high heels and he watched her hips sway as she went into the kitchen.

He stared at the wall for a long minute, his mind working overtime. What if it had been one of his brothers? He wouldn't have been there, to share in that experience, and that was not fucking okay.

He had to get back to Knight Ops, and that meant giving up Team Rou.

He'd done his best, and he couldn't even think of their losing McMahon as a failure on him. After all, shit happened. But he didn't deserve that team, and if he was honest, he was more than happy being second in command to his brother.

But there was one man who deserved to fight alongside those men—and he was going to speak with him as soon as he ate the sandwich that his beautiful woman was holding out to him.

* * * * *

Hawkeye eyed Sean warily as he took a seat across the restaurant table from him. A pot of coffee already sat there with two mugs, and Hawk was taking his black.

Sean added a bit of cream to his mug and poured it to the brim before speaking.

"I bet you're wondering why I asked you to join me for breakfast," Sean said.

"If this has to do with Elise, you'd better not be about to tell me you're leaving her. You break her heart, I break your legs." Hawk's dark eyes shot bullets through Sean.

"Not that. I love Elise, and I'm never letting her go."

"Good. She fucking needs a man like you."

Surprised, Sean sat back in his seat. "I'm glad to hear that from you. Your opinion means a lot to Elise… which means it affects me as much."

Hawk nodded. A platter of eggs and bacon with grits and home fries was set before him and the waitress took Sean's order before walking off again.

Hawk lifted his fork but didn't dig into the food. "Say what's on your mind. Neither of us are pansy asses."

"Okay. I want you to take over Team Rou."

It didn't seem Sean could have told him anything more shocking. Hawk's jaw dropped as he stared at him for ten full heartbeats.

"You're fucking kidding me."

"No. And before you ask, this isn't about McMahon. It was a horrible loss, but I made my decision before I even walked into that swamp with him."

Hawk set down his fork. "You want to give up the leadership of Rou." It wasn't a question.

Sean nodded. "I don't belong with them—not like you do. I belong with Knight Ops, and if you'll agree to take this promotion, I'll tell Jackson after I leave here."

"Does Elise know anything about this? Does she have something to do with you offering this to me?" Hawk's lips twisted in suspicion.

He shook his head. "She doesn't know anything. I thought it best to discuss it with you first. Will she have a problem with it?"

What he was asking was out of his comfort zone and almost galled him a bit. Sean was basically saying that Hawk knew the woman he loved better than he himself did. But he planned to remedy that for the rest of his life.

"It won't matter to her one way or another," Hawk said.

"Good. So, what do you say?"

"I say you're fucking reckless and a snot-nosed brat to throw a promotion back in Colonel Jackson's face."

Sean couldn't help but chuckle. "So we both know Jackson."

"Uh-huh. And he's gonna crush you like a bug, Knight. You're crazy, you know that?"

"Probably, but I know where my heart and loyalty lie, and I'm making the right decision for all parties concerned."

Hawk stared him down for a second. "Well, if you're passing the baton, who am I to turn it down?"

"This all depends on Jackson's final say, you know that."

"I know." Hawk picked up his fork again as if the conversation was over and everything was settled. "I'll take Rou, and gladly. They're my boys and I'll do right by them."

Sean felt the weight of that—the passing of the baton, as Hawk had said, with a show of respect for what Sean had done for that team. "It's settled then. I'll speak to Jackson as soon as I leave here."

"I might as well come with you to get the honors of the position." Hawk's teeth gleamed as he gave a cocky grin. He sobered. "You sure your old team will take you back?"

"Hell yeah. Family always welcomes the prodigal son back into its fold." He took a sip of his coffee with his own cocky smile.

Hawk chuckled. "Damn, boy, you're just right for this line of work. And for Elise. Take care of her, got it?"

"I plan to." For the rest of his life. The ring seemed to burn in his pocket.

"And Hawk?"

The man looked up from his meal.

"I hope you like nutria because those crazy fuckers are mad for it."

He licked his lips. "I'm feelin' a bit like having some barbecue right now."

Chapter Thirteen

Elise's palms were sweating. This had never happened to her before, and that must mean she was making the right choice, right? Sean made her heart beat faster and her knees quivery.

Not to mention her panties were constantly damp when he was around.

She slipped a dress over her head and eyed her shoe selection. Strappy sandals or little leather booties. Which would Bo choose?

She went for the sandals and was just buckling the small straps when the doorbell rang.

"I really need to get Sean a key," she muttered and hurried out of her room.

When she opened the door, she sucked in a sharp breath.

Holy shit, the man cleaned up well. Like GQ's sexiest man alive well. When she'd asked him to dress nice and come pick her up, she never would have imagined he had such great style. In a navy suit tailored to fit the man's hard body to perfection, a crisp white shirt and navy tie with dark red polka dots, he looked like he'd just stepped off the glossy pages. Even his white pocket square smacked of sexy.

She wet her lips, raising a groan from him. "Damn, baby." She sidled up to him and gripped his lapels, leaning in to inhale his cologne. "You look good."

"I don't think we'll be leaving the apartment tonight." He skimmed his hands over her breasts and down to her hips. Tugging her against him, he kissed her softly. In seconds, it exploded into passion and she drew back, panting.

"I... I really do have a surprise for you."

He gave her a crooked smile. "I have a couple for you too. The El Camino awaits. Do you have a handbag or something to put over your shoulders?"

"Nah, it's a warm night and I have everything I need strapped to my thigh."

His eyes bulged, and he reached for her hem. "Tell me you're packing heat, *cher*. That is so fucking hot."

"I guess you'll find out later. I'll just lock up." He stepped outside as she pulled the door shut. Then he took her elbow and led her to his car.

She'd never seen this side of Sean before. The fact that he could be that bayou boy and a suave guy dressed to the nines as well as a brilliant operative while acting as her personal bodyguard gave her a warmth that she'd never shake as long as she lived. She was so in love with him, she didn't know which way was up.

She didn't care either. She planned to love hard and never slow down.

After he opened her door and she slid into the leather seat, she watched him strut around the vehicle to get behind the wheel. He cocked a brow at her as he started the engine. "Where are we going?"

She took out her phone, which she'd already programmed with the destination. She pressed a button and the electronic female voice came on.

He gave her that crooked grin. "Aren't you clever? Okay, I'll follow your directions."

As they navigated the streets of New Orleans, he took her hand, his rough fingers stroking over the backs of her knuckles and sending images of him touching her all over into her brain.

By the time they reached the street where the inn was located, she felt breathless and so needy. He stopped at the end of the street and looked over at her. "Are you serious?"

She nodded.

"God, I don't deserve you." He rolled down the street and up to the inn. Silhouetted by the fading sun, sand and surf, it was the perfect place for her to try to prove how much she loved him. All. Night. Long.

"We're staying here?" he asked when he'd parked.

"Yes, for two nights. If you don't get called out."

"Or you don't."

She squeezed his hand. "I wanted to bring you back to where we started. It wasn't very long ago, but I feel like we should remember." Her throat clogged on the words.

"Oh *cher*." He unfastened his seatbelt to lean across the car and hold her. She wrapped her arms around him tight, holding on. After a long second, he said, "Let's go inside. I'd like to get this dress off you."

A laugh bubbled up her throat. "You just want out of that constricting jacket."

"I'm comfortable. This is like PJs to me. I can fuck in this suit if you want me to."

"Hmm." She traced the sharp lines of his shoulders and found her gaze lingering on the bit of tanned throat where the white shirt was buttoned. "I might take you up on that."

"Hmm." His eyes glowed with desire.

After they'd checked in and made it to their room — which happened to be the same room where they'd made love that first time, Sean closed the door with a predatory smile.

Trembling, she waited. What she was about to do wasn't something they taught women. Men, yes. But women were left out of this loop, and she was making it up on the fly.

She was jittery, her nerves snapping.

He approached her slowly, his muscular thighs stretching the fabric of his suit pants. Damn, she was nervous but just looking at him told her she was making the right decision.

"Sean." She took his hands and looked up into his eyes, mouth suddenly dry. "I wanted to bring you here because..."

He waited, searching her eyes. At this moment, she realized just how patient he truly was. It struck her that he'd make a wonderful father.

Heart overflowing, she struggled for words that she hadn't been able to rehearse because they hadn't come to her. But she had to find a way—she wanted this so bad.

"Sean, I love you."

"I love you too, *cher*."

"I mean I love you so much."

He nodded. "Same." His voice was gritty.

"I wanted to bring you here because it was where we started, and it hasn't been very long that we've been together, but in our business...

Well, there's no hesitation, is there? We have to take chances when they present themselves."

"Sweetheart, is this an operation?" he asked gently, ducking his head to hold her gaze.

Why was she so nervous? She needed to just blurt it out.

"I want to marry you. I mean, I want you to marry me."

He went still. After a deafening five heartbeats, he blinked. Her gaze locked on that spot on his throat only to see his Adam's apple bob hard up and down, looking about to cut through the skin.

"We never know what will happen tomorrow, and why shouldn't we grab onto what we've got and enjoy it every second we can?" Now she didn't know if she sounded persuasive or desperate. Maybe both. Her palms grew slick again, and Sean released them to wrap her in his arms.

When he pulled her against his chest, she felt his heart slamming hard. "Please tell me what you're thinking. I've never proposed to anybody before," she whispered.

A noise broke from him that made her pull back to look into his eyes. "Oh my God, Sean, you're going to cry!"

"Marines don't cry. But we do come prepared." He reached into his pocket and drew out a ring box.

She stumbled back, both hands clasped over her mouth. Butterflies hatched in her stomach and she didn't know how long she could remain standing. Shock took over.

"You… were going to propose to me tonight too?"

"You beat me to it, and I've forgotten all the pretty words I meant to say to you. But…" He dropped to one knee, the box cracked open to reveal a stunning diamond solitaire in platinum. He stared into her eyes. "Elise, will you be my wife? I love you. I'll never stop loving you. And I promise to work hard for you and do everything in my power to come home to you."

"Oh my God, Sean. I love you so much. Yes!" She stepped forward and hit her knees in front of him. He yanked her into his arms and kissed her, a deep, heartfelt kiss that warmed her entire body and started a thrum between her thighs.

As he slanted his mouth over hers, he caught her hand and slid the ring onto her finger. She broke away to gaze down at it.

"It's so beautiful."

"Not as beautiful as you, but I couldn't find anything that matched as well."

"I love it." They shared a grin.

"Now about this dress."

"We have dinner reservations downstairs, but I think we can miss it for this important meeting."

"Uh-huh." He eyed her breasts, making her nipples pucker.

She slid his tie through her fingers, cocking her head to the side as she considered how to go about unwrapping this extraordinary present. First thing she was going for was that yummy spot on his neck. She leaned in and opened her mouth over it.

He groaned and she felt him getting hard against her. Need sprang up, and she couldn't go slow. She ripped at his clothes. Working his shirt buttons and tearing off his tie. His suit lay crumpled on the floor and her dress topped the stack as he lifted her and walked to the bed, controlling her mouth like the master he was.

When he laid her down, she surged up to grip his cock. The velvet steel in her hand along with the shiny new engagement ring made her pause.

"All right, *cher*?"

"Yes." She went her lips. "I want to suck you." Without waiting for his response, she

264

shimmied down his body and swallowed him whole. Feeling the big man lose control under her tongue gave her a heady feeling. And when she lapped at his balls, he grunted and yanked her up the bed.

"Enough. I need to slide into your slick pussy."

His dirty talk fueled her fires. She parted her thighs in invitation and he didn't think twice before pressing his swollen head to her wet heat. He paused, holding her gaze. "I love you, Elise."

"Love you, Sean." She pushed her hips upward as he slammed into her, joining them, stretching her to the point of no return. Her mind shattered and she only felt. Sensation took hold and she bucked her hips, driving them to an end that had the walls vibrating just like the last time they'd shared this bed in this inn.

* * * * *

Sean couldn't quit looking at his fiancée. His bride-to-be. With her skin gleaming in the moonlight and stray grains of sand clinging to her shoulders, she was the most beautiful creature he'd ever seen. And her wearing his ring only compounded that feeling.

She brought her knees up to her chest, her hair caught by the Gulf breezes. They'd just made love on the sand and he was still hard. He couldn't get enough of her.

She turned her head, the long arch of her neck begging for his lips. "Why are you looking at me like that?"

"Just thinking you're beautiful." His Cajun drawl was more prominent, and she smiled. "And there's something else I wanted to tell you tonight."

She held out her hand and examined her engagement ring. "More than this?"

He nodded. Suddenly, he didn't know how she'd take hearing him say that he'd walked out on Team Rou—or that Colonel Jackson had been disappointed but gung-ho to have Hawk take his place.

"Sean, what is it? This is the start of our lives together, and I want you to always be honest with me."

He drew in a deep breath, scented with salt and Elise. "It's about Team Rou."

Her lips parted, and an expression of sheer worry crossed her beautiful features. "What about it?"

"I know you told me to take the position, but I've been thinking. It just isn't for me, and it's not only about McMahon, though God knows that was a hard loss." His voice broke and he took a second to collect himself.

She scooted closer on the sand and put her arms around him, offering comfort.

"But I guess it was that moment that started me thinking harder about my place. I always wanted a leadership role, but once I had it, I realized that being second in command is just as important."

She gaped at him. "Of course it is, Sean. Did you ever believe it wasn't?"

He shrugged. "I know I'm a crucial part of the team. Each of us is. But I've made some decisions and it affects you too."

"Okay…" She sounded worried now, and he smoothed a hand over her spine.

"I gave up Rou, Elise. And Hawkeye's taking over." He watched her.

She blinked and then a smile came over her face. "Damn, I bet he's thrilled about that. He was jealous as hell when they gave the team to someone else and then to you. It's where his heart is."

He stared at her. Did that mean his heart wasn't with Elise anymore, as her handler? That presented more worries for Sean about who was going to take over that role for her, but she was a strong woman and would be all

267

right no matter who fed her the information necessary to do her job.

"You're okay with it, then? With Hawk being leader?"

"Of course. He's a friend, Sean, but nothing more. You know that. So, does that mean you're back on Knight Ops again?"

He nodded, a smile tugging at the corners of his lips. When he'd made a group call to his brothers and Rocko, they'd raised a deafening cheer at the news. That had made him feel pretty damn good about his decision.

He flexed his arms around Elise, the only woman in the world for him and the center of his universe. "Thank you for being so damn supportive of me. I know it's not easy loving a man like me."

"Or a woman like me."

She was right—he'd go crazy each time she got an operation of her own.

He raised her chin with his knuckles to look into her eyes. "We'll handle it together. And we can always come back to this inn to reconnect."

She leaned in to brush her lips across his, the tenderness drawing all his love and need to the surface. He had to put his hands on her, bury his cock in her.

"I was thinking we could have our wedding reception here. Keep it small, just family. I'll invite my mother and her man."

"That sounds perfect, *cher*."

"More than perfect." She threaded her fingers around his nape and brought his head down for a lingering kiss that sealed the deal on their plans for the rest of their lives.

THE END

If you've enjoyed HEAT OF THE KNIGHT, I would love if you'd take a moment to leave a review. —Em Petrova

Em Petrova

Em Petrova was raised by hippies in the wilds of Pennsylvania but told her parents at the age of four she wanted to be a gypsy when she grew up. She has a soft spot for babies, puppies and 90s Grunge music and believes in Bigfoot and aliens. She started writing at the age of twelve and prides herself on making her characters larger than life and her sex scenes hotter than hot.

She burst into the world of publishing in 2010 after having five beautiful bambinos and figuring they were old enough to get their own snacks while she pounds away at the keys. In her not-so-spare time, she is fur-mommy to a Labradoodle named Daisy Hasselhoff and works as editor with USA Today and New York Times bestselling authors.

Find Em Petrova at empetrova.com

Other Indie Titles by Em Petrova

Knight Ops Series
ALL KNIGHTER

HEAT OF THE KNIGHT

Wild West Series
SOMETHING ABOUT A LAWMAN
SOMETHING ABOUT A SHERIFF
SOMETHING ABOUT A BOUNTY HUNTER
SOMETHING ABOUT A MOUNTAIN MAN

Operation Cowboy Series
KICKIN' UP DUST
SPURS AND SURRENDER

The Boot Knockers Ranch Series
PUSHIN' BUTTONS
BODY LANGUAGE
REINING MEN
ROPIN' HEARTS
ROPE BURN
COWBOY NOT INCLUDED

The Boot Knockers Ranch Montana
COWBOY BY CANDLELIGHT
THE BOOT KNOCKER'S BABY
ROPIN' A ROMEO

Country Fever Series
HARD RIDIN'

LIP LOCK
UNBROKEN
SOMETHIN' DIRTY

Rope 'n Ride Series
BUCK
RYDER
RIDGE
WEST
LANE
WYNONNA

Rope 'n Ride On Series
JINGLE BOOTS
DOUBLE DIPPIN
LICKS AND PROMISES
A COWBOY FOR CHRISTMAS
LIPSTICK 'N LEAD

The Dalton Boys
COWBOY CRAZY Hank's story
COWBOY BARGAIN Cash's story
COWBOY CRUSHIN' Witt's story
COWBOY SECRET Beck's story
COWBOY RUSH Kade's Story
COWBOY MISTLETOE a Christmas novella

Single Titles and Boxes
STRANDED AND STRADDLED
LASSO MY HEART
SINFUL HEARTS
BLOWN DOWN
FALLEN
FEVERED HEARTS
WRONG SIDEa OF LOVE

Club Ties Series
LOVE TIES
HEART TIES
MARKED AS HIS
SOUL TIES
ACE'S WILD

Firehouse 5 Series
ONE FIERY NIGHT
CONTROLLED BURN
SMOLDERING HEARTS

The Quick and the Hot Series
DALLAS NIGHTS
SLICK RIDER
SPURRED ON

Also, look for traditionally published works on her website.

Printed in the USA
CPSIA information can be obtained
at www.ICGtesting.com
LVHW011616090724
785028LV00008B/369

9 781717 464170